Just One Fling

A Kingston Family
Dirty Dare Story

NEW YORK TIMES BESTSELLING AUTHOR

Carly Phillips

Dear Reader:

Just One Fling takes place one month after Just One Taste. If you haven't read Taste, there is no impact on your reading enjoyment.

If you have read it, this timing information helps fill in the gaps. As always, all Carly Phillips books stand alone.

Happy reading!
Xo Carly

Chapter One

WINTER CAPWELL STEPPED into the penthouse, where she was meeting with Nikki and Derek Bettencourt, her heart pounding hard in her chest. She was about to reveal a secret she'd been keeping since she moved into Nikki's building. Now it was time to come clean, and Winter was nervous as hell.

Asher Dare, Nikki's fiancé, opened the door to the apartment he and Nikki shared, but Winter's gaze went directly to the siblings waiting for her. Nikki, with her long, dark hair, and Derek, his hair a touch lighter, shared similar facial features. Including the green eyes that met Winter's gaze, a hue so like her own.

"Hi, Winter. What's going on?" Confusion etched Nikki's face, along with concern.

Winter didn't blame her. She and Nikki had spent a lot of time together after the former model had returned from Asher's Eleuthera home, where she'd stayed after a devastating scandal. That had been where a twenty-one-year-old Nikki had coupled with Asher, the billionaire owner of Dirty Dare Spirits and the Meridian Hotels. But in all their time walking

1

Winter and Nikki's dogs, meeting for coffee, and getting to know each other, Winter had never hinted at hiding a secret. One that included Nikki and her brother, Derek.

Before Winter could answer, Asher spoke. "Winter asked to talk to you both privately, so I'm going to leave you alone. I'll be in my office if you need me."

"No, stay," Winter said. If she'd learned anything about Nikki, the younger woman could handle Winter's news but would want all the support she could get to process the information.

Nikki looked from her fiancé to her brother, who shrugged, obviously as lost as she was.

But Asher cut Winter a look that warned her if she hurt his fiancée, she'd answer to him. Nothing surprising there. It didn't matter what Winter revealed, Asher would look out for Nikki, making it easy to see why she'd fallen for the brooding, protective man. Though Winter preferred his more light-hearted, sexy brother, Harrison. But now was not the time to think about her hot summer fling.

Asher rested his palm on Nikki's back, and she leaned into him, proving Winter's instinct correct in asking him not to leave.

"Let's sit," Asher suggested, for which Winter was grateful.

Her legs were trembling as much as her insides. He

led them into the overly large family room, and they all chose their places, Asher and Nikki on one end of the soft, taupe-colored suede sofa, Derek in a black leather club chair.

Winter took the opposite end of the couch and tried to relax, but her leg bounced up and down, nerves consuming her.

"Okay, time to talk," Derek said. "What's happening here? Why did you need to see us?"

Nikki tilted her head. "Winter?" she asked, clearly wanting answers, too.

Winter swallowed hard and met their curious stares. "I wanted to tell you this a while ago, but first came your... scandal," she said to Nikki, hating to bring up such a painful time. "And then the break with your parents. Then you and Asher got engaged, and I didn't want to ruin your happiness. There was never a good time."

Placing a hand over her stomach, Nikki drew a deep breath. "We've grown close, Winter. The fact that you're a reporter made me uneasy at first, but you promised me you had no interest in me or my family as interview subjects."

"And I don't," Winter rushed to reassure her. "But I do have another kind of interest." She glanced down at her manicured nails, studying them instead of facing the duo just yet. "I'm just going to lay out the truth,

3

but bear with me while I explain." She rubbed her hands on her black leggings, gathering her courage. "Here goes. I moved into your building on purpose so I could meet and get to know you."

"What the fuck?" Derek exploded, protective of his younger sister.

"You'd better keep going with the explanation," Asher said, his jaw clenched tight, his hands clasped around Nikki's.

God, Winter almost wished she had someone who cared enough to bolster her now. But that wasn't the life she'd been given, and despite this news, it had been a good one so far.

"I was raised by my mother. No father in the picture. My mom always told me she didn't know who he was, and because we were such a tight unit, I let it go. Mom was independent, and I was okay not knowing. Then…" She pulled in a much-needed breath. "About a year ago, Mom was diagnosed with cancer. Shortly before she died, she told me who my father was."

It wasn't easy to speak over the lump that rose in her throat whenever she talked or thought about her mother. They'd been so close, and the loss had been, and still was, devastating.

They sat in wary silence, waiting for Winter to continue.

So she did. "After the funeral, I was alone, and I

couldn't stop thinking about what my mother had told me. By then I was a reporter, and my desire to prove who my father was outweighed my mom's wish for me to leave things alone. I started with one of those ancestry tests, just to see if it revealed anything. It came back, connecting me to…" She looked from Derek to Nikki. "Both of you."

"Holy shit," Asher muttered.

"I need to think," Derek said, running an agitated hand through his hair.

Nikki blinked. "Wait, Derek. Remember that Christmas we bought each other one of those ancestry tests? We knew Mom would have a fit, so we sent them to your friend's house and took them there?"

Derek nodded, and his furious expression eased a bit as memory lit his eyes. "Our mother wouldn't want anything out in public or online that would call attention to our father, the senator, or impact his potential run for the White House."

Yes, Winter knew all too well how badly Collette Bettencourt wanted to be First Lady and how far she'd go to make that happen.

"The test came back with the information we already knew about our ancestry, and I forgot all about it." Nikki removed her hand from Asher's grip and waved it in the air as she spoke, growing more excited as she recalled the connection to Winter's story.

Derek leaned forward. "I checked off the boxes that would notify me if someone signed up who was related to us. But a couple of years later, my email was hacked, and I had to get rid of the account. I re-signed up for as many places as I could remember, but I forgot about the ancestry site." He shook his head in wonder.

"But your names were listed," Winter said.

Derek ran a hand through his hair and groaned. "And you found us. But I still want a DNA test as proof."

"I figured you would."

Derek's demand wasn't insulting. Winter wanted the same thing.

"I have a friend who's a pediatrician," he went on. "I'll ask him to pull strings and get it rushed through the lab."

She couldn't expect to announce she was the illegitimate daughter of Senator Corbin Bettencourt, who represented NY State in the US Congress and hope to be immediately believed.

And she wasn't finished with her story, either. "Umm, there's more." She figured she might as well air all her dirty laundry at once.

Derek placed his arms on his thighs and groaned. "Let's hear it."

She sighed because the story didn't paint her

mother in the best light, but they deserved to know. "As you already figured out, my mother and your father had an affair. It was after you were born, but before Nikki," she said, looking at Derek. "Mom knew the senator was married. From what she told me, he never made any promises, and she didn't ask for any. When she found out she was pregnant, she had every intention of raising me on her own. But your mother found out."

Winter swallowed hard, deciding to leave out *how* Collette discovered her husband's mistress was pregnant for another time. "She confronted my mother, swore her husband's *slut* wouldn't ruin their political aspirations, and paid her to have an abortion."

Nikki gasped, but Winter forged on, needing to purge herself of the information and see what the siblings chose to do afterward.

"Obviously, my mother didn't have the abortion but did keep the money. She moved from New York to a small town in Maine and raised me there. And that's it in a nutshell."

Silence settled over the room as everyone processed Winter's words and she held her breath, worried about what Nikki and Derek would think of the mother Winter had loved.

What Winter found most interesting was that neither Nikki nor Derek questioned that *their* mother would do such a thing. Given the fact that Collette Bettencourt had belittled Nikki for not living up to her expectations while manipulating her daughter to do as she wanted, perhaps it wasn't a shock.

Nikki had cut ties with her parents after they'd ignored her in public, humiliating and hurting her badly. It worried Winter that their father was capable of such cruel behavior, making her wonder if she wanted to get to know the man.

"Assuming your story is true, and I believe it probably is, what do you plan on doing with the information? The revelation could bring down a politician and create a massive scandal," Derek said, his gaze on Winter's.

"Which you and Nikki, especially Nikki, have had enough of." Winter blew out a long breath. "I never had any intention of hurting either one of you. I just wanted to know my family because the truth is, I have none."

She forced herself to meet Nikki's gaze, only to see her half-sister's eyes were glassy, and she stared at Winter as if trying to work through all she'd learned.

Winter bit down on the inside of her cheek. "I've gone back and forth on whether I want to know my father. I'm aware of how badly your parents have treated you," she said to Nikki. "And *you* told me how you were manipulated into an engagement." She shifted her attention to Derek.

"It's not exactly a secret," he muttered.

Winter nodded. "Would it be a problem for either of you if I confronted them? Once we had the test results back, I mean." Though she asked them both, she couldn't tear her gaze from Nikki's. "You're my friend," Winter said, her voice plaintive because she *liked* Nikki. "I don't want to lose you."

What Winter really wanted was to gain her as a sister, but it was up to Nikki whether or not she wanted that, too.

"I feel the same way about you. I can't say this is easy to digest, and I agree with Derek. We should get proof." Nikki pulled her hand from beneath Asher's and rose to her feet. "I want you to know, no matter what the results show, I believe *you think* we're half-sisters. And if the samples match and you want to confront my parents, I understand. I needed to do the same thing."

Nikki's words eased the weight in Winter's chest, and the next thing she knew, Nikki was hugging her despite not knowing for sure if they were related.

ONE WEEK LATER, the test confirmed Winter's mother's claim. Three days after that, Derek and his fiancée, Jessica Cavanaugh, invited Winter to Jessica's house for dinner, along with Nikki and Asher, so they could get to know one another better. They were curious about Winter's mother and how Winter had grown up. Despite the preexisting friendship, the evening began awkwardly, but by the end of the night, they were laughing and had made a start toward becoming a family.

And the next weekend, Winter, with her new brother and sister by her side, showed up at their father's home with the DNA test in hand. The senator had broken down and cried when he found out he had another daughter. Collette, on the other hand… to say she hadn't taken the news well was an understatement. First, she'd been shocked and in denial. When faced with the DNA test results, she'd begun to scream and yell that everything she'd worked for would be destroyed and all because Winter's bitch of a mother hadn't done as she'd promised.

She'd actually gone after Winter, attempting to attack her physically, until Derek had grabbed his mother around the waist and pulled her back. The senator stared in shock. Nikki yelled at her mother to calm down and discuss things like a rational human being. Finally, when nothing would make Collette stop her ranting, Winter had left with Nikki. Derek stayed to try and talk sense into his mother.

By the time Winter had walked into her apartment, she'd seen for herself how weak her father had been and seemingly still was. He'd called her later, having gotten her number from Derek, and had been full of apologies for not knowing about her. For letting Collette rule his life.

Winter didn't know what kind of relationship she'd ultimately have with the man who, on paper, was her father. Nikki wasn't speaking to either parent. Derek was also done with their antics. And yet Winter was still curious about Corbin Bettencourt.

RISE AND SHINE, America. I'm Erin Sawyer, and this is our political news of the week wrap-up. New York Senator Corbin Bettencourt has resigned his seat in the US Senate and stepped down from politics to, in his words, focus on his family.

His resignation comes after the revelation that he sired an illegitimate daughter he claims to have known nothing about. His wife, Collette Bettencourt, allegedly paid off her husband's mistress to have an abortion. Instead, legal secretary Juliana Capwell, now deceased, took the money and raised her daughter far from DC in New Westminster, Maine. DNA tests have proven the senator's daughter, freelance reporter, Winter Capwell's, claim.

The former senator has already filed for divorce from his wife and moved out of their New York home. According to a source who preferred to remain anonymous, both Bettencourts are said to be estranged from their children, Nicolette and Derek, and the former senator has yet to bridge the gap with his newfound daughter. And now for the latest budget dispute on Capitol Hill...

Chapter Two

One Month Later

H ARRISON DARE STEPPED into the ballroom at the Meridian NYC Hotel which was heavily decorated for Halloween. He scanned the room, telling himself he was admiring the décor and *not* looking for the elusive woman he couldn't get out of his head.

Winter Capwell, a brilliant reporter and a sexy siren in one delectable package. They'd met at his company's Hampton offices this past summer for an in-depth interview with the K-Talent Productions team. The sparks had been immediate and *hot.*

He hadn't felt that kind of connection with anyone before. Not even with Sharon McNally, his one-time girlfriend, a woman with whom he thought he'd had a future. Instead, she'd used him for his Hollywood connections, betrayed him, and taught him the value of no emotional entanglements.

He shook off those memories and returned to thinking about Winter. They'd tried to keep things professional, but their chemistry had been too strong to ignore. Add in the fact that she'd asked him many personal questions, and since they'd spent so much time together, in bed and out, a part of him felt like he'd revealed things to Winter, the woman, not the reporter.

He knew better, of course, and had kept his head when answering, giving her the practiced answers necessary to keep his privacy.

For a man who liked no strings, Winter had seemed like the ideal woman. She hadn't been interested in a relationship any more than he had, and they'd agreed to keep things casual while she was in the Hamptons interviewing his team this past summer.

It was perfect.

She was perfect.

A hookup that was nothing more than a warm body in his bed. He told himself she would satisfy a need, the same as any other female he'd been involved with in the past. Except Winter had quickly become *more,* and Harrison didn't know what to make of that.

True, his siblings were settling down, with the exception of Zach. But Harrison had ruled out marriage and kids for himself. Any thoughts of having his own family had been derailed by the girlfriend he'd hoped to propose to. Sharon had no problems with the notion of using the casting couch to secure better roles despite having a serious boyfriend at the time.

Winter had come into his life, and she'd been an unexpected treat, but he'd kept to the plan, and their time together came to an end when the interview had. These days, Harrison's production work kept him busy, as did his large family, most of whom would be here tonight.

With a groan, he looked around the room. Since Winter was nowhere to be found, he focused on the event itself. The Kingston and Dare families used any excuse to raise money for charity, and tonight was no exception. The funds donated would go to Future Fast Track for foster children, the charity Aurora, married to Harrison's brother, Nick, had founded to help kids about to age out of foster care.

The event was full, the entry fee and plate cost were high, and the décor was elaborate thanks to Harrison's sister, Jade, the event coordinator for the Dare family Meridian Hotels. Keeping with a spooky theme, onyx and purple linens covered the tables. The centerpieces consisted of black pumpkins and white skeleton heads surrounded by long twigs, purple feathers, and similar-hued flowers. His sister had outdone herself tonight.

"What's got you looking like a proud papa?" Dash Kingston, lead singer of the band The Original Kings, strode up to him, holding his one-year-old son, Freddie, in his arms.

"Proud *brother*. I was just admiring Jade's talent," Harrison said, adjusting his bow tie. No matter how many parties and award shows he attended, he still hated the feeling of being strangled by the damn thing.

"You're looking uncomfortable," Dash said with a smirk. "Who are you supposed to be, or is that penguin suit just a way to avoid putting on a costume?"

"Bond. James Bond," Harrison said in a practiced British accent. He let his gaze skirt over the other man's jeans and Original Kings band T-shirt. "What about you?"

"Kingston. Dash Kingston. Rock star." Dash laughed, knowing he was bending the rules by going as himself and clearly not giving a damn. His sister, Aurora, wouldn't give him too much of a hard time. "And this is Freddie Mercury. Give the crowd a wave," he said to his son.

The little boy with his mother's blue eyes, his father's dark hair and famous dimple in one cheek, waved a chubby hand. He gripped a blow-up guitar in the other and kept knocking Dash in the head with it.

"Good job!" Dash grinned indulgently at the young toddler. "Freddie pulled off his mustache earlier. Didn't you, little man?"

Harrison shook his head and laughed. "Freddie's the greatest rock star ever," he told the boy, a deliberate dig at Dash, both because his son wouldn't understand and that's how his and Dash's friendship rolled.

Dash frowned at Harrison and moved the guitar that had bopped him in the nose. "Let's go find your mom." He leaned in so Freddie couldn't hear. "Cassidy's dressed as Madonna's character from some 80s movie. She's hot." He chuckled and moved the guitar away from his face again. "Talk to you later, Bond."

The boy banged his plastic instrument against his dad's head as they strode away.

"He's a good father," Asher's familiar voice said, his brother sneaking up beside him.

"He is." Harrison turned to his oldest sibling, who wore a pair of Levi's and a black mock turtleneck.

Knowing Asher was the most serious of them all and the least likely to dress up, Harrison took an educated guess at his costume. "Steve Jobs?"

Asher nodded.

Their family had agreed to surprise each other tonight, and no one knew what anyone else was wearing. Since Jobs, Apple's co-founder, was known for sporting that same outfit day in and day out, it wasn't a hard guess. The Apple CEO had once been quoted as saying he owned over one hundred Issey Miyake black turtlenecks.

Asher gave Harrison a once over. "Bond?" he guessed.

Harrison grinned. "Who else?" Knowing Asher wouldn't be here alone, Harrison glanced over his brother's shoulder in search of his fiancée and hopefully her sidekick.

"Winter and Nikki stopped at the restroom. They'll be here in a few minutes," Asher said.

Harrison opened his mouth to protest, but Asher shook his head. "Don't bother. We both know you're looking for Winter."

Caught, Harrison clamped his mouth shut.

"She came by tonight so the women could help each other with their costumes," Asher said.

"Of course." *The women weren't just as close as sisters,* Harrison thought. *They were sisters.* And the news had been the secret that had been eating away at Winter during Asher and Nikki's engagement party over Labor Day weekend.

When Winter finally admitted her relationship to the Bettencourts, Harrison had understood why Winter had been so preoccupied that night. Why she'd had too much to drink and no doubt why she'd ended up in Harrison's bed again. After they'd agreed the end was… the end.

"There they are." Asher raised a hand, capturing his fiancée's attention.

Nikki waved back, but Harrison only had eyes for Winter, entranced by her beauty. A little black dress hugged her curves while black heels accentuated her long legs. Legs he'd had wrapped around his waist and wanted there again.

He bit back a groan, staring instead at her beautiful features, her eyes covered by dark-tinted, black-framed sunglasses. Her dark, shoulder-length hair was pulled back with a comb on one side, revealing a multi-strand pearl necklace with a diamond brooch against her soft skin.

Audrey Hepburn, *Breakfast at Tiffany's*, reincarnated.

He drew in a sharp breath, causing Asher to chuckle.

"Fuck you," Harrison muttered, sliding his gaze to Nikki. It was safer to look at his brother's fiancée. It would give his sudden hard-on a chance to subside before the women crossed the room.

The sisters had obviously planned to coordinate because Nikki was also dressed as Holly Golightly from the movie, but unlike Winter's dressy outfit, Nikki opted for the bedroom scene costume. She wore a sleep shirt on top, tasseled earrings, and an eye mask pushed up on her forehead. On her feet, she'd slipped on pink, fuzzy bedroom slippers.

No doubt Asher would be escorting her home to remove that nightshirt as soon as they could politely escape. Considering Harrison wanted to do the same to Winter, his guess was beyond an educated one.

The women made their way across the increasingly

crowded ballroom and walked up to them. Nikki slid into Asher's waiting arms, snuggling against her fiancé.

Facing Harrison, she grinned up at him. "Hi, Harrison."

He kissed her cheek before turning to… "Winter." He smiled, his gaze lingering on hers as he did his best not to ogle her sensual curves.

"Harrison." She looked him over, her emerald gaze darkening, telling him he wasn't the only one affected. "Are you going to a premiere afterward or is this your costume?" she asked in a husky voice.

He gave her a mock bow. "James Bond at your service."

She let out a laugh. "Oh, I love that."

He did his best not to preen under her admiration. "You two ladies look gorgeous." But his pulse only ran fast for one of them.

Nikki laughed. "It's fun. I'm not surprised you know who we are, being an actor and all."

He inclined his head. "*Breakfast at Tiffany's* is a classic."

"But not everyone knows the movie by name. I've been asked a few times already," Nikki said.

A few seconds of silence followed, during which Nikki's gaze shot from her sister to Harrison.

"Asher, would you come with me to get a drink?" she not so subtly asked her fiancé.

"Of course. Anyone else want something?" Asher asked.

"I'd love a club soda if you don't mind?" Winter's hand went to her stomach, and Nikki's expression turned to one of concern.

Harrison narrowed his gaze, also worried. "Are you okay?"

"I didn't eat much today. I'm just a little lightheaded."

"Still?" Nikki's lips turned downward in a frown. "Okay, well, we can grab you some appetizers, too. They might help. Be right back." Nikki and Asher walked toward the bar across the room, and Harrison decided to use the time alone with Winter.

"Is that all that's wrong? Lack of food?" He'd hate it if she were sick.

She nodded. "I think so. That and stress," she admitted.

Given her life lately, he understood. "How have you been, *really*?"

She drew in a deep breath and exhaled, then propped her sunglasses on top of her head.

Harrison studied her more closely, seeing now that her porcelain skin was pale.

She blinked as her eyes adjusted to the lack of dark lenses. "That's so much better than staring into darkness." She tipped her head toward an empty corner of the room. "Let's move over there to talk."

Understanding she wanted privacy for this conversation, he grasped her elbow and led her to where she'd indicated.

"Anyway," she said once no one was walking past them. "I'm okay. It helped that the DNA test came back quickly, and Nikki and Derek were understanding." She pulled her lower lip between her teeth, and he withheld a groan, wanting to taste those plump lips himself.

"I'm glad they took it well," he said.

She nodded. "They did. Mostly. Derek was upset I didn't come clean as soon as I grew closer with Nikki, but I'm learning he's protective of his sister." She stepped back and leaned against the wall.

"Understandable." Nikki had been through a lot, and that was before the sister revelation.

"But they both get why I waited. I was looking out for Nikki. First the scandal, then the engagement. It never seemed like the right time. And I didn't want to burst her bubble with life-altering news."

The reminder of the engagement party had her blushing because that was when they'd indulged in a repeat of the summer. Something he couldn't regret, and he hoped she didn't either.

He and Winter hadn't spoken for a couple of weeks, but the minute she'd walked into the party, he'd sensed something was bothering her. Knowing how independent and capable she usually was, he'd sensed a vulnerability underneath that typically strong journalistic exterior.

He'd asked her what was bothering her, but she hadn't been in a talking mood that night. Since he'd volunteered his Hamptons home for the party, they'd wound up naked in his bed. He'd intended to find out what was wrong in the morning, but when he'd woken up, Winter was gone.

Harrison had taken the hint and left her alone. Until the bombshell news broke.

She drew a deep breath and let it out again. "I'm just grateful I have family now."

Her soft smile did something weird to his insides. Jesus. *She got to him on so many levels,* Harrison thought. Sex was easy. Emotions... just fucking weren't. He'd shut his down after Sharon had hurt him, but Winter had dug in deep. Though he'd tried to get her out of his head, hitting the bar his brother, Zach, owned and going out with the guys in search of fun and women like he had in the past, his dick hadn't been interested.

Because other women weren't Winter.

"I'm happy for you," he said.

Coming from a large family—four adult siblings from his father and mother, and another four with his father and Serenity, his former nanny—he knew the importance of having people in his corner.

He hadn't appreciated what he had when he was younger. After he'd graduated high school and before leaving for college, he'd been *discovered* by a talent agent while hanging out on a movie set courtesy of a friend's father. Going across the country had appealed to him because home was chaotic. He had four young siblings, and he needed space and quiet to figure out who he wanted to be. He wasn't shallow, but the Hollywood lights had beckoned. He'd loved the life… until it grew old, and he missed his family.

"Thanks. That means a lot that you're happy for me." Winter smiled but she appeared tired. There were dark circles under her eyes that she'd tried to hide, and it was obvious the wall she was leaning against held her up. He hoped Nikki and Asher returned quickly with food.

"What about the senator?" he asked, keeping the conversation flowing. "Have you heard from him since you told him who you were?"

She winced. "And trashed his marriage and chances for the presidency?"

Harrison touched Winter's shoulder, offering comfort. "You didn't cause any of that. *He* had the affair, and his wife did the rest. You just told your truth."

She nodded. "I appreciate you thinking that way. And Harrison, thank you for checking in… you know, after it all happened."

"I wanted to make sure you were okay." In fact, he hadn't been able to stop thinking about her and wondering how she was holding up under the strain.

"We're back!" Nikki and Asher strode up to them. Nikki had appetizer plates in her hands while Asher held the drinks.

"Oh, good. Winter, here." Nikki held out a plate to her sister. "This is tea-smoked duck, whatever that is."

Winter's eyes opened wide, and she shook her head. "No thanks." Her pale face turned even whiter. "I'm really not feeling well. I need to go home."

"I can take her so you two can stay," Harrison offered, placing a hand under her elbow for support.

"No. I—"

"I'll go," Nikki cut Harrison off. "Nobody wants to get sick with anyone but family or a good friend around."

Harrison tried not to be offended by the comment, knowing what Nikki meant.

"We'll take her," Asher said. "My driver is waiting."

"No!" This time, Nikki's voice rose. "You stay. Your family is here. Let me handle it." She patted Asher's shoulder and turned to her sister. "Come on. I'll get you home, make you toast and jelly..." Her voice trailed off as she led Winter away.

Concern filled Harrison as he watched them walk off. He glanced at his brother. "What the hell was that about?" he asked.

Asher lifted his shoulders, looking as confused as Harrison felt. Nikki had seemed determined to get her sister out of the room.

"Women," Asher muttered, and Harrison agreed.

WINTER HAD TAKEN one look at the duck, smelled the hors d'oeuvre, and needed to get away. She rushed to the ladies' room, Nikki right behind her. Thank goodness the outer area was empty. At the sink, she turned on the cold tap and placed her wrists beneath the running water. The cold sweat and nausea began to pass.

"Are you okay?" Nikki put a gentle hand on Winter's back.

"Yes. Sorry. I didn't mean to scare you. I just needed some air." She shut off the faucet and picked up the hotel monogrammed paper towel, and dried her hands, tossing it in the trash.

Turning, she faced her sister.

"Are you sick?" Nikki asked.

"I don't think so." Winter hadn't lied to Harrison when she'd told him the same thing. "I didn't eat a lot today, and I skipped lunch. And the food we nibbled on while dressing didn't do much to fill me up. That's all."

"Really." Nikki studied her, hands on her hips. "Then what was your excuse the other morning when you bailed on our coffee date because you were exhausted and not feeling well?"

"I—"

"Was exhausted and not feeling well," Nikki finished for her.

Winter lifted her shoulders in a half-hearted shrug. "I didn't realize it was becoming... a thing."

Nikki patted the lounge chair beside the one she'd settled into, and Winter sat down. "Maybe you need to go for blood tests? See if anything is going on? You're nauseous, tired..."

Hearing the list, Winter nodded. She'd been busy finishing writing and turning in an article that was due and stressing about the upheaval she'd caused the man who was her father, not to mention worried about Nikki and Derek despite their assurances that they were fine.

Winter hadn't had much time to think about herself or how she was feeling. Now that she gave her issues serious consideration, she realized there were other symptoms.

"What is it?" Nikki asked into the silence.

Winter swallowed hard. "Well, I've gained some weight because this little black dress is a lot tighter than I remember," she said, wishing she could loosen the material. "And my boobs hurt," she admitted.

"Holy shit! Winter, could you be pregnant?"

She sat up straight and stared at her new sister, suddenly aware the symptoms she was experiencing *could* point in that direction. "I... I'm on the pill." She rubbed her suddenly throbbing temple. "But I had strep before your engagement party and was on an antibiotic the week prior." She thought back and tried to remember. "I think I was still taking it the night of the party... and I slept with Harrison, but we used protection. I know we did."

"You drank. A lot. Are you sure?"

She nodded. "But if the pill was ineffective because of the antibiotic and condoms aren't one hundred percent. Oh God," she moaned.

She peeked through her hands as she faced her half-sister, who, at twenty-one years old, was more perceptive than Winter was at twenty-four. "I wasn't just busy with work and my crazy exploding life, I was in deep denial." She began to breathe too rapidly, the all too likely possibility settling in.

"Okay, so forgive me, but I have to ask. If you are pregnant, are you sure it's Harrison's?" Nikki's squinted eyes and apologetic expression said it all.

Winter nodded. "There's been nobody since... I can't even remember right now. Definitely before I ever met Harrison." Which made her moan again because her potential baby daddy? He didn't want kids at all.

She'd asked that very question during their interview session where she'd channeled her inner Barbara Walters in asking uncomfortable questions her audience would want to know the answers to.

"What do you see in your future? You come from an extremely large family. Is that what you want, too? Lots of kids?" Winter had asked.

He'd laughed, showing off those sexy dimples. "Oh, hell, no. I have four adult siblings and four younger ones. I grew up in a loud, busy house. I'll take my single life of peace and quiet, thank you."

She swallowed over the bile threatening to rise in her throat.

"Come on." Nikki stood, grasped Winter's hand, and pulled her to her feet.

"Where are we going?"

"To your place, but we're stopping at a drugstore and buying a few home pregnancy tests first."

At the same moment, the bathroom door opened, and a group of women walked in, laughing and talking loudly. Any further personal conversation would have to wait.

"I can do it all myself," Winter told Nikki. "No need for you to miss the party. You're all dressed up and everything."

Nikki rolled her eyes. "I know you're accustomed to doing things alone but get used to me being around. I wouldn't leave you now if you paid me to go."

Winter managed a smile, and gratitude filled her. The last thing she wanted was to find out whether or not she was pregnant by herself. She just wouldn't have thought to ask her new sister to stay.

"Thank you," she whispered.

There was a chance she wasn't pregnant. The stress surrounding her was real. She had her biological father trying to talk to her and the press attempting to interview *the former senator's illegitimate daughter.* If it turned out Winter *was* carrying Hollywood's Hottest Playboy's baby, there would be no place for her to hide.

Chapter Three

WINTER AWOKE, AND her new reality came rushing back. She was pregnant. This time, when her stomach churned, she wasn't sure if it was morning sickness or pure panic. Her dog, Panda, who slept beside her on her own pillow, realized Winter was awake, walked across the mattress and began to paw her shoulder.

"I know. You want to go outside."

She licked her cheek, and she smiled.

Forcing herself out of bed, she pulled on a pair of pants and a heavy sweatshirt, stopped in the bathroom, and then hooked her leash and led her out for her morning walk.

As she took her along their regular route, she had time to relive every moment of last night. She and Nikki had stopped to buy the tests, and they took Asher's car and driver to her apartment. Winter followed the instructions and then they waited while the endless minutes passed. When her phone timer went off, they'd both stared at the identical results across three different brands.

Nikki had freaked and began pacing the room, and

ironically, Winter had had to calm her sister down. Needing to be alone to process things, she'd convinced Nikki to go home to Asher, who had left the event not long after they had. He was not a party person, and it was no surprise he hadn't wanted to stick around once Nikki left.

Knowing there was no way Nikki could keep the news from her fiancé, despite him being Harrison's brother, Winter had agreed to let her confide in him, but extracted a promise to let Winter tell Harrison herself. Asher was a rational guy, and she trusted him to keep quiet unless he thought Winter was hiding the truth, something she'd never do.

With Nikki gone, Winter had taken Panda for her last nightly walk and returned home, washed up, and climbed into bed. Though she'd expected to toss and turn, to her shock, she'd slept like a baby. Pun definitely intended.

Now, walking in the cool morning air, Panda finished her business and Winter returned to the building, waved to the doorman, and rode the elevator to her upstairs apartment. She fed the dog and headed to the bathroom to take a shower.

She turned on the faucet so the water would heat up and turned to face the mirror. Lifting her nightshirt, she looked at her flat stomach. Though there was no bump, she knew from last night's dress her shape had shifted already. There were a lot of changes to come, and she needed to mentally prepare.

She blew out a deep breath and pulled the material over her head, then stripped out of her pants and underwear and stepped beneath the running water.

As she soaped up with her coconut-scented gel, then washed and conditioned her hair, she faced one simple fact. She was single and pregnant like her mother had been, with a baby daddy who didn't want kids. Except in her mother's case, the senator hadn't wanted kids with *her*. He'd already had a son when Juliana realized she was pregnant.

Winter's situation was different. Harrison might not want a family, but he deserved to know. As for Winter herself, she might be surprised but she already knew she planned to keep her baby. She admired her mother for raising her alone and wanted to make her proud by emulating her in the same way. Given her trust issues, Winter had never been certain whether or not she'd have children. She hadn't planned to marry any more than she'd thought about having a baby on her own. But now she would be.

She rinsed off and shut off the water, then stepped out of the shower, where Panda waited to lick the droplets of water off her legs. Winter wrapped her hair and her body in plush towels, her mind immediately returning to her being pregnant.

Thank goodness she was financially secure, though it had been hard won. Her early years in journalism and interviewing had consisted of beating her head against male-dominated walls.

The professors in school and the arrogant bosses she'd interned for had seen her as naïve, good for getting coffee and doing *their* research, never giving her a real shot to show her talent.

The men she'd casually dated within the industry had been even worse, just as demanding and using her contacts and abilities for their own gain while also expecting her to put out after they split the dinner bill.

Then came her lucky break. She'd gone to a fundraising event where Erin Sawyer, a well-known news anchor and Winter's idol, had been speaking. Winter had seen the journalist alone in the hallway and approached her, gathering her courage to ask how a woman could move up in their profession.

The anchorwoman had looked her over, pulled out her card, and told Winter to be in her office the next morning. Just like that, she'd gained a mentor, and as time passed, Erin had become not just a friend but a surrogate mother. She'd taught Winter that women help women, a lesson she'd never forgotten and always paid forward, and it was Erin whom Winter had trusted to break the story of her father, the senator. Knowing Senator Bettencourt planned to quit his position and acknowledge Winter as his daughter, Winter and her siblings had agreed to put the story out on their terms.

Winter's career would enable her to support herself and a baby. Undercover reporting had never been her gig, so she worked from home unless she was doing an extended set of articles like she'd done with Harrison and his partners. Despite this pregnancy being unexpected, Winter couldn't be in a better position to raise a child by herself.

She walked to her bedroom and pulled on a pair of silky lounge pants and a matching top. Her hair fell past her shoulders in wet waves, and she squeezed out the water, deciding to let it air dry. She would be okay, something she knew she'd have to keep telling herself as time went on. Her mother had been an independent woman, and Winter turned out the same way. She'd learned to make fast decisions and stick by them. Though she was thrown by her new circumstances, she already knew she could handle it.

The next step, she wasn't so sure about. How to tell Harrison he was going to be a father. When the phone rang, she'd been so lost in thought she jumped at the sound.

She glanced at the screen to see it was her doorman calling. "Hello?"

"Mr. Harrison Dare is here to see you, Ms.

Capwell."

She blinked in surprise. "Umm…" She thought she'd have time to prepare herself and figure out what to say, but maybe it was better this way. Spontaneity, and she'd get the truth out there. No living with it like she'd done with knowing she was Nikki's sister and keeping the news to herself. It was better to get it out there and let the cards fall where they may. "Send him up, please."

She had no time to primp, not that it should matter. She and Harrison had ended their relationship when the interviews had, and their Labor Day oops had been just that. An oops.

One that tied them together for the foreseeable future. She'd like to say she didn't have any lingering feelings for the man, but that would be a lie. Even after she'd left the Hamptons, Harrison Dare had never left her mind, which explained why she'd fallen back into bed with him so easily.

Winter wasn't someone who slept around. Her relationships weren't deep, but she cared about the men she had sex with. The problem was, nothing about Harrison had been about just sex, no matter what they'd agreed upon at the time.

So, did she care that he wasn't going to see her at her best? Of course. But she had no choice. Drawing a deep breath, she went to let Harrison in.

She opened the door, and he stood waiting, one arm on the doorframe.

"Hey," he said, and of course, *he* looked good.

He hadn't shaved and his scruff was dark and sexy, making her remember how it felt abrading her thighs.

Forcing her thoughts away from trouble, she glanced into his deep-blue eyes. "Hi. What are you doing here?" she asked.

He shoved his hands into his front pants pockets. "You left so suddenly last night. I wanted to check on you."

Ignoring the twisting in her stomach at the concern in his voice, she rushed to assure him. "I'm okay."

"It's not a stomach virus?" He winced. "Something I didn't think through before showing up on your doorstep." He grinned, and she did her best not to focus on those dimples. It wasn't the time.

"Definitely not a stomach bug," she said. "And I appreciate you stopping by." He'd saved her a trip, not that she'd mention that.

Opening the door wider, she moved aside so he could step into her small entryway. "Come into the family room," she said, shutting the door behind him.

She led the way, and his footsteps followed her to the casual room with her large plum-colored sofa.

Ever the gentleman, he waited for her to sit before

lowering himself beside her. "How are you feeling this morning?" he asked.

She swallowed hard. "Better. For now."

He narrowed his gaze. "What does that mean? Is there something seriously wrong?"

"No." Instinct kicked in, and she grabbed his hand. "No. But there is something going on, and it involves you."

He turned so his knees rubbed against hers. "I don't understand."

She gave herself one last pep talk, assuring herself she could get the words out. "Last night, I found out I'm pregnant," she said. "And before you ask, you're definitely the father."

He stared at her for a long moment, his mouth open in disbelief, and something else she couldn't decipher in his wide-eyed gaze.

"Pregnant." The word shot from his mouth and ricocheted around them. "You're sure?"

She nodded. "As sure as three home tests can be." She ran her hand up and down the silk material of her lounge pants and stared at her pink nails against the light blue material.

Pink and baby blue, she thought, trying not to let a manic laugh escape.

"Fuck." He looked like he was about to lose his breakfast, which would have been comical if things weren't so serious.

"That sounds about right." She waited, giving him time to think. Processing wouldn't happen quickly. She wasn't sure she'd managed to do that yet, either.

But the longer he sat in silence, rubbing his jaw with one hand, frowning and shoving his fingers through his hair, she realized he wasn't taking this well at all. Not that she thought he would.

She drew in a deep breath and let it out slowly before speaking. "Look, you don't need to worry about anything. I can handle it all myself." It's what she'd expected to happen, anyway.

"Whoa." He glanced up at her, his brows snapping together. "I've had thirty seconds to think since I heard the news. It doesn't help anything to make assumptions about what I will or won't do."

Her chest grew tight, and she sighed. "I'm just going by what you told me. *Your words* during the interview, when I asked if you wanted kids or a family and your answer was a definite *no*."

"Fair enough," he said, and her throat threatened to close at his easy agreement.

So she'd been right. He didn't want children and her pregnancy had him spiraling. Deep down, she'd obviously been hoping for some sort of reassurance, but he hadn't offered any. *Typical man*, she thought, eyeing him warily.

He ran a hand through his hair once more and his eyes held a dazed expression. "But that doesn't mean I'd shirk my responsibility. I was raised better than that."

Responsibility. She blinked at the cold word and drew back her shoulders. Being an obligation was the last thing she wanted to be to anyone, especially a man.

"*We*," she said, placing her hand over her flat belly. "Are not some burden you have to take care of, and I don't want you around because you feel obligated. My mother raised me alone, and I can do the same thing with my baby."

He worked his jaw, his frustration clear. "It's not a matter of obligation. I helped get us into this situation, and I'll do right by you and the baby."

She rose, needing to put space between them. "Fine, Harrison. You do whatever it is you think you have to do."

She didn't have to like his attitude, but she'd accept whatever he offered because his support was best for her baby. He'd probably throw money at her and disappear from her life, and it would be smart of her not to expect anything more.

"I'm not sure what else you want me to say."

She didn't know either.

Jaw clenched, he stood, and the distance between

them couldn't grow any bigger. "I... just give me some time to process the news and figure things out. I feel like I've just been hit by a fucking freight train," he said, running his fingers through the hair he'd turned into a spikey mess.

Unexpected tears sprung to her eyes. She'd blame them on hormones, but she knew this conversation had pushed her over the edge and she turned to the window, not wanting him to see her emotional up-heaval.

"Winter—"

She waved away his concern with one hand. "Just go. I have things to do," she lied and didn't turn around again until he'd walked out and she heard the door shut behind him.

★ ★ ★

HARRISON STARED AT the four empty bourbon glasses on the table at his brother Zach's bar and grill. The Back Door was named after the entrance located in the rear of the building, with a nod to his sibling's computer hacking skills. Then there was the Urban Dictionary meaning, giving the place triple entendre significance. Zach found it amusing.

Harrison leaned back in his chair and waved until the server, Raven, a pretty brunette who flirted with

Zach and vice versa, walked over.

Harrison lifted his empty glass.

She shook her head. "Your brother cut you off," she said, picking up one empty glass at a time and placing each on her tray.

"Come on. I need it." If he kept drinking, the words, *I'm going to be a father*, would stop swirling around in his head.

She shrugged, sympathy in her eyes. "Sorry. Take it up with management." She sashayed over to the bar, hips swaying, and stepped behind it, where she said something to Zach, who nodded and gave Harrison a hooded look before turning to another customer.

From the moment Harrison had walked in, chosen a table, ordered, and refused to discuss what was bothering him with his sibling, Zach had watched him warily from behind the bar. So, Harrison wasn't surprised when the rest of his siblings strode in and pulled up chairs around his table.

Zach had clearly called for an intervention. Making his way across the room, the traitor joined them. He dragged a chair from another table, turned it backward and sat down, straddling the seat.

Asher placed his hands on the wooden table and studied Harrison. "Okay, let's have it. What's got you drowning your sorrows?"

"I need one more drink, and then I'll tell you,"

Harrison muttered.

Zach rolled his eyes and nodded at Raven across the room.

"I left my wife and kids at home," Nick said. "And by the look of you, it's a good thing I did. But you'd better start talking."

Jade, Nick's twin, nodded in agreement. "Leah wanted to come, but I had a feeling this wasn't the time to see her uncle. I'm here for you," she told him, squeezing his hand.

His gaze drifted from the twins to Zach and then to Asher, the father figure of them all. It wasn't that their dad, Michael, was a bad father. Not at all. He'd just had his hands full after Audrey—mom of the siblings sitting here now—had walked out and all but disappeared.

When Harrison was six, their father told them he'd gotten word she'd died by suicide. The truth still caused him deep pain, yet it was hard to think of Audrey as his mother when Serenity, once the nanny and now his stepmom, had always filled that role.

Asher had stepped up to help. Of everyone, Harrison hated to disappoint him the most. But from the serious scowl on big brother's face, Harrison had a feeling he already had. No doubt Nikki, who'd probably known about Winter's pregnancy since last night, had filled him in.

Harrison couldn't put it off any longer. "You all remember I was seeing Winter Capwell this summer?"

"Is that what they're calling it these days?" Nick asked with a chuckle. As brothers, they always gave each other shit.

Jade nudged her elbow into his side. "Shut up. Go on, Harrison."

He drew a deep breath, preparing to say the truth out loud for the first time. "Winter is pregnant, and I'm the father."

"Oh, Harrison!" Jade reacted first, and she covered her mouth with one hand.

"Shit," Zach said as Raven set down Harrison's drink and discreetly walked away.

Asher's gaze remained steady on Harrison, confirming he already knew.

Nick clenched his hands together on the table, clearly having lost his amusement now that he knew the facts. "As someone who had a child and didn't find out about it for five years, the upside here is you won't miss out on being there for Winter and your kid."

Harrison groaned. Of course, Nick would immediately put himself in Harrison's shoes and have a different feeling about the situation. When Nick was younger, he'd been in Florida for college spring break. He'd had a one-night stand with his now-wife, Aurora.

They hadn't exchanged last names, and she'd had no way to find him.

At the time, she'd just aged out of foster care and had been living in the back room of the diner where she worked. She'd been alone, penniless, and pregnant before her life had finally taken a positive turn. The Kingstons had discovered she was their illegitimate sister. Linc Kingston had gone to Florida to find her and bring her home. Four years later, luck had brought Nick back into her life. So yeah, he'd missed out on a lot, and he'd have given anything to have been there from the beginning.

But Harrison? When Winter told him she was pregnant, he hadn't acted like an upstanding guy despite his proclamation of having been raised better. Actually, when he thought about it, he'd been a dick and should have at least left her with more concrete reassurances.

He was about to pick up his bourbon glass when Jade grabbed it out of his hand. "Cut it out and grow up. If you're this thrown by the news, how will you handle the reality?" she asked, her hand cupping her pregnant belly.

Also, an accidental pregnancy. And how had Jade's baby daddy handled the news? Knox—clearly a better man than Harrison currently was—had chased Jade to Asher's home in the Bahamas, where she'd fled in a panic. Because *he'd* been in love with Jade and hadn't been willing to lose her or their child.

Harrison wasn't in love with Winter, but he wasn't over her, either. After their summer fling, he'd wanted more even after they'd gone their separate ways, which wasn't his normal M.O. In the past, he always walked away without looking back.

Kids might not have been on his radar, but if he had to go through the experience with anyone, it would be Winter. He rubbed his hands over his eyes and muttered a curse, knowing he needed to get his shit together.

He'd wallowed in self-pity long enough. "You're all right."

He gestured for Raven, who walked over.

"What can I get you?" she asked.

"Coffee, black. And—"

As if reading his mind, Raven reached out and picked up the glass she'd only recently put down and walked off, hips swaying again, except this time, Zach's gaze remained on her sultry exit.

Harrison knew better than to call him on it. Another time, maybe. Right now, *he* was in the hot seat, and his family had a point. It was time to get his head out of his ass.

"Let's start from the beginning," Asher said. "When did you find out?"

"This morning. I went to check on Winter since she'd left the party last night because she wasn't feeling well. She told me. And I..." God, he didn't want to admit to all of this.

"Please don't say you asked if the baby was definitely yours," Zach said into the silence.

Harrison rolled his eyes. "No, that's something you might do. But I did fuck up."

With distance, some alcohol, and the memories of how his siblings had gone through similar situations, he realized he'd let his panic override being a decent human being.

"What did you do?" Asher asked.

"I was in shock, and at first, I didn't say anything."

"Understandable," Zach, the only single one, said.

"Then?" Nick asked.

Harrison swallowed hard. "When I was quiet for so long, she told me I didn't have to worry about a thing. She already knew how I felt about having kids, and she was prepared to handle it herself." His gut twisted at the memory.

"Wait." Asher held up a hand. "You two discussed having children? I thought this was a casual relationship?"

"It was, but Winter interviewed me, remember? She's good at her job, and she dug deep. She asked about how I saw my future, if I wanted a family." He scrubbed a hand over his jaw.

"And you said?"

Harrison winced. "Something along the lines of, *'Oh, hell, no.'* Then I mentioned growing up in a large, noisy family and said that was why I preferred my single life of peace and quiet."

He pressed his palms against his dry eyes while a chorus of groans echoed around the table. He blinked the room back into focus as Jade rose to her feet.

She walked over and smacked him in the head. "Idiot," she muttered.

"Hey! Winter was a reporter. That's my standard canned answer. If I said anything different, I'd have women lining up to have my babies."

"Swelled head, much?" his sister asked before walking back to her chair and sitting down.

"I know how bad that sounds, but it's the truth." It was just hard to believe how much he'd enjoyed that lifestyle when he'd arrived in LA and again after he'd broken up with Sharon.

The women throwing themselves at him at A-List parties, hitting on him in bars and restaurants, rubbing their fake tits against his arm. And when he'd been chosen as Hollywood's Hottest Playboy? They'd lined up outside his apartment. No joke, when his family visited him, they couldn't even go out for dinner because he'd have been swarmed by females and photographers.

"Okay. Let's focus," Asher said. "I'm going to have to deal with my fiancée, who happens to be Winter's sister, so I want to understand. Tell me you reassured Winter you'd be a stand-up guy?"

"The way Knox did for me?" a very pissed-off Jade chimed in.

Harrison's mouth grew even drier than it had been. "I told her that regardless of my feelings, I wouldn't shirk my responsibilities. That I was raised better."

Asher groaned.

"I know, okay? I didn't handle things well." He'd let Asher and the rest of his siblings down. He'd also disappointed himself. He could only imagine what his father, Michael, and stepmom, Serenity, would say.

But worst of all, he'd hurt Winter so much that by the end of the conversation, she'd refused to look at him. Even before turning away, she'd already felt the need to protect the life inside her *from him*, placing her hand on her stomach and refusing to be anyone's burden. Something he'd all but told her that's what she and their baby were to him.

"At least he knows he fucked up," Zach said, making Harrison realize while he'd been kicking his own ass, they'd all been talking around him.

Pushing out of his chair, he rose to his feet, taking a second to gain his balance.

"Where are you going?" Asher stood up, too.

"Home to sober up. I have a flight to LA in the morning for meetings. I'll be gone for about a week. I'll text Winter from there and make sure she knows when I get back, we need to talk."

Time away would give him a chance to pull himself together and have a rational conversation planned out for when he returned.

"I'll drive you," Asher said, walking over and slinging an arm around his shoulder, causing Harrison to relax.

No matter what any of them did wrong, they were family, and he was lucky to have each person that was here worrying about him. If the situation were reversed, he'd do the same for them.

But his time for dicking around and turning to alcohol as a solution was over. He was going to be a father, and he needed to grow the fuck up.

Chapter Four

AFTER HARRISON WALKED out, Winter ran to the bathroom, and she'd been sick. Since she was between assignments, she'd taken advantage and climbed into bed with Panda and slept until Nikki called to say she was coming over. The dog had been nudging her anyway, so she'd climbed out of bed, walked Panda, and waited for Nikki, who had arrived ten minutes ago with pints of ice cream she'd picked up on the way over.

Winter's stomach was still off, so she decided to save the ice cream for later.

"Stop pacing," Nikki said, walking over to the kitchen table and setting down a cup of chamomile tea. "This has no sugar and a drop of milk. It will help your stomach and hopefully relax you."

Taking a seat, Winter sent her sister a grateful look. She wrapped her hands around the warm mug and sighed. "Thank you." She lifted the cup and took a delicate sip, happy when she didn't burn her tongue. "What brings you by?"

Nikki grabbed a bottle of water from the fridge and joined Winter at the table, taking a chair across from her. "I was worried. You didn't answer my first three calls today."

"Sorry. It wasn't an easy morning." Winter took another soothing sip of tea. "I told Harrison about the baby."

Nikki met her gaze. "How did he take it?"

"Oh, about as well as I expected from a man who said he didn't want kids." Her stomach twisted at the reminder.

Nikki tipped her head to one side. "He said that?" Her hands curled tighter around the water bottle, obviously angry on Winter's behalf.

"Well, to be fair, he said it during our interview this past summer, but he didn't deny it today. Do you know how he feels about it?" Winter asked.

Nikki shook her head. "Sorry."

Winter swallowed hard. "It's fine. I told him I'm prepared to handle it on my own."

Though Nikki winced, Winter wasn't as freaked out by the prospect. Scared? Yes. But she had her mom as an example, and she'd make things work.

"How did you leave things?"

Winter took a moment, focusing on her palms against the ceramic mug, letting the warmth seep into her. "He said he wouldn't shirk his *responsibility*." She all but spat the word. "And I do not want to be some man's obligation." The thought made her sick, and the pain of his words stayed with her all day.

"Oh wow. I'm going to kill him." Nikki rose from her chair, stepped over, and wrapped her arms around Winter's shoulders, and she leaned her head into her sister's embrace.

For so much of her life, it had been her mom who provided all the hugs Winter needed. Erin had been a big support too, but over the last year, with her mom gone and Erin living in Washington, DC, Winter had been so alone. Having Nikki was slowly giving her the comfort she'd been denied.

"Actually, I'm sure Asher's letting him have it right now."

"What?" She pulled away and looked up, causing Nikki to step back and meet her gaze.

"Umm…" Nikki nibbled on her lower lip. "Asher got a call from Zach. Harrison was at the bar, and something was clearly wrong, but Zach couldn't get it out of him. Zach asked all the siblings to come by."

"An intervention. Lovely." Winter shook her head. "So they're all there talking about me?"

"More like they're giving Harrison shit for his attitude. It's what they do. Something happens, and it becomes a family affair."

"I wouldn't know anything about that," Winter said and finished her tea, needing the comfort she found in a drink her mom used to make for her.

Nikki went to step forward again, and Winter shook her head, not needing another hug. "I'm fine," she assured her sister. "And I'm so grateful to have found you and Derek. At least this little one will have an aunt and uncle who want to get to know him or her." It was so odd to think she was having a baby, she mused, still unused to the idea.

Nikki settled back into her chair. "Umm, however Harrison acted today, I promise you and your baby will have a huge family for support. After they met me on the island, before Asher and I were officially together, the Dares all but adopted me. You're going to find yourself one of them, too."

At the thought of strangers invading her space and wanting something from her she wasn't ready to give, Winter felt her walls going up. "I don't know. Look how long it took me to reach out to you?" She was very used to being on her own.

Nikki rolled her eyes. "That was because you were holding onto a huge secret. This is different. I didn't mean to scare you. Just let things play out. Harrison isn't a bad guy. He's a scared, shocked man. And no, I'm not defending him." She held up a hand before Winter could think to object. "I'm Team Winter, always."

At that, Winter's eyes filled. "Thank you." She rose, and this time, Winter initiated the hug. "I'm grateful for you."

Before Nikki could answer, Winter's cell rang. She stepped back and looked at where it was plugged in on the counter. The name, *Corbin Bettencourt*, flashed on the screen. She hadn't been able to type in the word *Dad* when her biological father had given her his phone number.

She glanced at her sister and knowing how Nikki felt about the man, decided not to take the call.

"You can answer it. I don't mind," Nikki said.

"It's… our father."

Nikki wasn't on speaking terms with either of her parents and her lips pursed before she asked, "Do you two speak often?"

When it came to their biological father, sometimes Winter and Nikki discussed him, but more often they didn't. Nikki's wounds of neglect were still fresh. And Winter was trying to understand how she felt about the man who'd had an affair with her mother but let his wife lead him around by his balls at the expense of his legitimate kids.

There was no other kind way to think about the situation, Winter thought. "No. He calls though. He wants to get together and talk."

Nikki nodded. "Do you mind if I ask why you haven't done that yet? I mean, you went to a lot of trouble to meet me and eventually tell us we're related, not to get to know your father."

Winter sighed. "Because I don't like how he treated you, and I need to decide if he's for real or if I'd be letting someone toxic into my life. And now I have a baby to think about." She pressed her hand to her stomach, something she could see would become a habit.

Nikki rubbed her hands together before meeting Winter's gaze, her own eyes sad. "I think he's a weak man but not a bad one, if that makes any sense."

It did, and Winter nodded.

"You showing up and revealing my mother paid yours off to abort his child behind his back opened his eyes. Just because I'm not ready to let him in again doesn't mean you shouldn't." Nikki managed a smile Winter knew was forced. "You'd be starting fresh. It's not the same thing as me getting over being emotionally hurt as a child and as an adult."

Winter blew out a long breath. "One thing I know. I'm going to be a much better parent than he was to you."

Whether Harrison would be a part of said parenting? She had no idea.

OCCASIONAL TRAVEL TO LA for auditions was part of

Harrison's job. He had business meetings to further
K-Talent's stable of both screenwriters and actors, and
friends out west he liked to catch up with. On this trip,
Cassidy and Sasha wanted his opinion on a lead before
they made an offer, and they had no desire to leave
their spouses. Harrison was always the one called on
since he was unattached and unencumbered. That was
about to change.

But while he was here, he had a job to do and
there were secondary roles he was looking to cast as
well. They had seen the video tests, but nothing was
better than a firsthand impression.

In the past, he'd never wanted to rush back to
New York.

He did now.

He didn't like how he'd left things with Winter and
hadn't slept well since she'd told him she was pregnant, his nonchalant attitude and casual words ping-
ponging in his head.

He'd sent her daily text messages asking how she
was feeling and receiving well-deserved, one-word
answers. He consoled himself with the knowledge that
the week was almost over. Today he had two auditions
to watch, one with a nepo-baby whose father was an
award-winner and the other, a well-known actor in his
own right. After lunch, Harrison would view a handful
of actresses for secondary roles and then Asher's jet

was waiting to take him home.

He sat in a comfortable chair in the conference room of K-Talent's LA offices along with the casting director for the movie. Lena was chewing gum and talking loudly on the phone, ignoring Harrison as she checked in on clients. They waited for the first audition to arrive, and he couldn't help but think about how everyone's path to stardom was different.

In his case, he and his friends had been hanging around a movie set, the cast on their lunch break. Harrison had been goofing around, acting out the role in front of his pals. He'd always found memorization easy, so after a morning of listening to the same scene over and over, he'd had the words nailed.

He'd performed, having no idea an agent was watching. Before that moment, acting hadn't been on his radar. Once in Hollywood, he'd booked a spot as an extra on a TV show, then his first movie, and suddenly the stars aligned. His first part exploded overnight.

A knock sounded on the door and the first audition walked in. After that, the morning ran smoothly, and soon they broke for lunch. He walked across the street to the sandwich shop, knowing he'd run into fans on the way. He graciously signed a couple of autographs and paused for a selfie with a mom and her daughter who'd seen and loved the indie movie he'd made, the one which had earned him an Academy Award nomination.

Sandwich in hand, he walked to a small park and ate, keeping his head down and enjoying the weather and sunshine before he returned to the office.

The waiting room was filled with talent, and he wove his way through the crowd toward the doors leading to the interior offices.

"Harrison? Harrison!" A voice he hoped never to hear again called for his attention.

Clenching his teeth, he turned to see his ex-girlfriend, Sharon, in the waiting area.

When they'd met, he thought she was a sexy woman. Three years younger than him, she was confident, poised, and he'd found it impressive how she was willing to mingle with people and push where others might hold back. It was only when he'd been smacked in the face with the truth of her betrayal that he saw her for who she really was.

In the years that followed, each time he ran into her, she seemed more aggressive. She'd obviously crossed into desperate territory, as her outfit told him she was trying too hard. She wore a tight turquoise dress, one he'd heard his brother's wives call a bandage or body-con style. Her tits were larger and obviously new. Her heels were high, her tan fake, and her makeup overdone.

"Harrison! It's so good to see you," she said, walking over and wrapping him in a floral-scented hug, her long brown hair brushing his cheek.

He stepped back and out of her reach. He couldn't say he was glad to see her, but he wouldn't be rude. "Hi, Sharon. Listen, I can't stay and talk. I'm needed back in the office." He turned to head inside, and she stopped him with a hand on his arm.

"What?" he asked.

"I'm auditioning, and I was hoping you could put our past aside and consider me. For old times' sake."

Lena opened the door leading to the offices and poked her head out the door. "Harrison, are you ready to begin?"

"Coming," he assured her, relieved to have been given a legitimate excuse to leave. To his ex, he said, "You can audition like everyone else."

"But we haven't had a chance to catch up," Sharon said on a whine, clearly unhappy.

Ignoring her, he walked away and took the encounter as a lesson to check the list of who was coming in the next time he sat for auditions. At least he'd have been prepared to deal with the viper. And that's what she was. Someone who'd had no problem betraying him.

He sat through the afternoon auditions, unsurprised at the number of people waiting for a chance to try out for a small role in their next movie.

The hours until he could leave dragged, but he gave every actress his full attention and took notes on each. Sharon walked in last. As she acted opposite someone who read the other role, she lost herself in the performance. As much as he hated to admit it, she'd nailed the part, not that he'd tell her as much. He'd give his opinions to Lena and his partners.

"Thank you," Lena said to Sharon when she finished. "We'll be in touch with your agent."

Sharon smiled widely and blew him a kiss he ignored before she turned and walked out.

"And that's it for the day," Lena said as she closed her iPad and put all her personal things into her bag. "I have to run across town to another meeting. We'll reconvene by Zoom or FaceTime and discuss our top choices?"

"Sounds like a plan." He had his notes jotted into his phone, not that he'd forget whose performances he'd liked.

"See you," Lena said.

"Bye, Lena."

She hefted her long strap over her shoulder and walked out.

Harrison was more than ready to call a car to take him to the Van Nuys airport, where the jet was waiting.

He pulled out his phone and opened the Uber app just as the conference room door opened, and Sharon stepped inside.

He tapped in the request for a ride and put the phone on the table. "Sharon, Lena said she'd be in touch, and she will."

"I left my bag." She pointed to the purse he hadn't noticed at the edge of the table.

He waved, indicating she should take it and go, and he walked a good distance away. *Self-preservation,* he thought, but she followed until she was beside him, stepping into his personal space and wrapping her arms around his neck.

"I've missed you," she said, pressing a kiss to his cheek and rubbing her breasts against his chest.

He felt nothing. No stirring, no desire, nada. "I can't say the same."

She pouted at his obvious lack of interest and her pursed, injected lips weren't pretty. "I was hoping that while you're here, we could... I don't know, revisit the past?"

"No," he said, tone firm.

She expelled a huff of air, her frustration obvious.

"Sharon, give it a rest." He reached around his neck in an attempt to untangle her arms and managed to step away. He took a much-needed breath free of her cloying scent.

A calculating gleam entered her eyes, and she straightened her shoulders, sticking out her firm breasts for him to notice. "Well, if you don't want to try again, I bet I can at least convince you to give me that role."

God, she'd changed, and it wasn't for the better. He refrained from rolling his eyes. "Good to see you're still trying to sleep your way to the top," he said, ignoring her slitted gaze. "And for the record, this behavior isn't going to get you a part in the movie, no matter how talented you are." If anything, he was now against giving her a shot.

"You think I'm talented?" Her voice rose, her surprise real. As if she'd been pulling this behavior for so long, she no longer considered the possibility of *earning* a part based on talent alone.

"It doesn't matter now. There's no way I want to deal with you in any way."

"That's not fair, Harrison." Fake tears welled in her eyes. "If I gave a good audition, me trying to get you back should have nothing to do with hiring me."

As if knowing he needed saving, his cell rang. He was too far away to easily grab the phone, but grateful for the interruption. "Hey Siri, answer the phone on speaker. Hello?"

"Harrison?" a sweet, feminine voice asked.

He closed his eyes and groaned. Of all people, he

hadn't thought she would call him. "Winter, hi."

"Why can't I see you?" she asked.

She was FaceTiming him. *Now?*

He wasn't sure his luck could get any worse, making him wish he hadn't turned off the announcement of incoming callers. At least then, he wouldn't have answered.

He and Sharon rushed for his phone at the same time, but she nabbed it first, turning the screen around so she could talk to Winter. "Hello, Harrison is busy at the moment."

"Who are you?" Winter asked.

"Hand the phone over, now," he ordered through gritted teeth. When Sharon didn't comply, he snatched it out of her hand and turned it toward him. "Winter, I'm sorry. Auditions just wrapped up, and *she* was just leaving. She grabbed my phone before I could."

Winter looked beautiful. No longer pale, her face was made up in a subtle yet sexy way. Red lipstick coated her full lips, she'd pulled her hair back in a sleek ponytail. She was everything Sharon wasn't, making him realize what a moron he'd been when he was younger.

"Interesting," she murmured. "I didn't realize watching auditions meant ending up with lipstick on your cheek. Unless you were playing the opposite role?"

"No, he wasn't," Sharon spoke up unhelpfully.

For the first time, he caught sight of himself in the small corner of the phone and groaned, rubbing the pink marks off his skin and wondering if he could fuck things up more than he already had.

He could only imagine what Winter was thinking. Probably that he'd escaped to LA after learning the news and was fooling around with other women while she was in NY dealing with an unexpected pregnancy.

Not that they were a couple. And he didn't owe her loyalty, but she deserved to feel like she mattered. And she did, more than she realized.

More than *he'd* realized. Her silence told him it was his turn to speak. "It's not what it looks like." The words were lame, and he cringed.

From where she leaned against the wall, Sharon snickered, and he shot her a glare.

"It's none of my business and I shouldn't have mentioned it," Winter said in a cool voice.

That first part might be true, but her perception of him had dropped even lower, and he wanted a fucking do-over for this day.

"Is everything okay?" He wouldn't say, *with the baby*, and give Sharon any ammunition over him. "What's going on?"

"Everything is fine, and it wasn't anything important," Winter said. "I should go."

Dammit. She'd called and now he'd lost her.

His ex was smirking as she gathered her purse from where she'd left it on the table. Sharon's grin told him she'd gotten her revenge for him turning down her advances and refusing to consider her for the part.

"Winter, I'll get back to you when I'm in the car on the way to the airport," he promised.

"You don't have to. I'm fine," she said and disconnected the call.

Sharon paused, her hand on the doorknob. "She was pretty. Too bad you blew it." She flung open the door and stalked out of the room.

"Oh, for fuck's sake." He ran his hand over his face before grabbing his phone.

The car was outside waiting to take him to the airport, where he could get on the jet and spend six hours figuring out how to make things right with Winter.

Chapter Five

Winter sat in the waiting room of the obstetrician's office. She'd called all over the city to try and get into a doctor quickly, wanting to confirm the home tests and learn what she needed to do to keep herself healthy. Every office she called was booked out, so Nikki had asked Jade and Aurora, who were both pregnant, to use their pull and make a call to try to get Winter in to see their doctor sooner. Apparently being a Kingston and a Dare had serious pull because two days later, Winter was here with Nikki by her side.

Her sister tapped her foot on the carpeted floor and glanced around. Winter followed her gaze, taking in the chairs filled with pregnant women, many with their uncomfortable-looking significant others.

"You still haven't told me why I'm here and not Harrison. I thought we'd talked things through, and you agreed he should have the chance to be with you."

Winter shrugged. "Let's just say I decided not to ask him." He'd texted while he was gone to check on her and because she appreciated the effort, she'd worked up the courage to FaceTime and invite him to join her today. She cringed at the reminder of the reason she'd brought her sister along instead.

Nikki narrowed her gaze. "What happened?"

"What makes you think something happened? Couldn't I have just changed my mind?"

She sighed. "Just tell me so I can sic Asher on him." A smirk lifted her lips.

Winter laughed. "You'll do no such thing." But she might as well tell Nikki the truth. "When I called Harrison to video chat, a woman answered his phone, and when I finally saw his face, he had lipstick on his cheek."

Nikki's eyes opened wide.

"He said it wasn't what it looked like, but come on. How trite is that?" Winter shrugged. "Anyway, it doesn't matter."

The fact was, while she'd been home worrying about his reaction to their baby and debating on how much to let him share, he'd been in LA, thoughts of her forgotten while he was busy doing some woman during auditions.

"It doesn't matter," Winter muttered.

But jealousy burned through her at the memory, and she shook off the useless emotion. She didn't want to feel that way about him. Harrison had been the perfect man for her because they were in agreement. Neither wanted a serious relationship, and that hadn't changed.

"Look, I know I have no hold on him, and he didn't do anything wrong, but seeing him in action made me realize Harrison didn't ask for this." She lay her hand over her belly.

Winter was just his *obligation*, as he'd said.

"Harrison didn't want this baby." And he didn't want her. "So I wasn't about to make a fool of myself by asking him to come to the appointment."

Nikki narrowed her eyes and pursed her lips, silent, obviously lost in thought.

"What is it?" Winter asked.

"Harrison said it wasn't what it looked like?"

Winter nodded.

"Well, I believe him." Nikki placed a hand on Winter's arm. "Listen, he's changed from his younger days. Asher told me he doesn't bed hop like he did when he first arrived in LA, so there's only one explanation for what you saw."

"Which is?" Winter asked skeptically.

"I*t wasn't what it looked like.*"

Before she could respond, her name was called, and she turned to see a nurse standing in the doorway to the exam rooms.

"That's me." Grabbing her sister's hand, she rose, and together they walked inside, leaving all thoughts of Harrison, and that other woman, behind.

Harrison called, texted, FaceTimed, and showed up at Winter's apartment building. She hadn't answered the phone, her *read texts* option was off, so he had no idea if she'd seen his message, but he'd bet she was ignoring him. And the doorman told him she wasn't home. He called Nikki, but she didn't answer either. Frustration rode him because he needed to sit down with her and discuss his involvement in both her pregnancy and their child's life.

When the direct route to Winter failed, he called his brother and somehow convinced Asher to tell him where to find the women. They were at Winter's first obstetrician appointment, and Harrison muttered a curse.

He had no doubt *that* was why she'd called him. To extend an olive branch and invite him to join her. Then she'd gotten a glimpse of his lipstick-stained face and decided he wasn't serious enough to be all in when it came to their baby.

Persuading Asher to give him the doctor's address hadn't been easy. Asher had insisted that if Winter wanted him to know, she would have told him. And Nikki would throttle him if he got in the middle of their issues.

Harrison tried reminding Asher that they were

brothers, Asher had informed him *fiancée trumped brother*.

"Would *you* want to miss your baby's first doctor's appointment?" he'd asked.

Asher had texted him the address.

Harrison walked into the office off Park Avenue. All sets of eyes turned his way, and most widened the moment they recognized him.

Shit.

A quick glance told him Winter wasn't in the waiting room, which meant she'd probably been called into the back. He was lucky enough that when he'd spoken to Asher, he hadn't been late for the appointment.

Harrison stepped up to the front desk where an older woman was on the phone, and he waited anxiously for her to notice him. When she finally glanced up, her lips parted in a surprised O. "You're... You're... Harrison Dare! Oh my God."

He leaned in on one elbow, giving her his full attention.

"Can I help you?" she finally remembered to ask.

"I'm here to see Winter Capwell. I was supposed to bring her today, but I was running late, so she came with her sister. Think you can let me in to surprise her?"

She furrowed her eyebrows together. "Oh, I don't know. It's against protocol. Let me go back and ask her."

That wouldn't work. Winter would probably have him thrown out. "This really needs to be a surprise." He treated the receptionist to his patented, big-wattage grin and turned on the charm. "Can you please help a guy out?" he asked with a wink.

She leaned in. "Will you give me your autograph?" She blushed as she asked.

"Sure thing." One signature later on an envelope, the nearest white paper she could find, and she led him to a room with a closed door and left him there.

Two nurses walked past. Both stared. A patient exited a room, noticed him and did a double take. So much for slipping in unnoticed.

Drawing a deep breath, he knocked on Winter's exam room door. A female doctor opened the door, and her gaze met his. After the requisite eyebrow-raising, she pulled herself together. "And who are you, besides Hollywood's Hottest Playboy?" she asked.

His face heated as it usually did when that stupid moniker came up.

"He's the baby's father," he heard Winter speak, followed by a heavy sigh. "You can let him in," she said, and the nervous knot in his stomach eased.

"Well, I was just leaving so Ms. Capwell can get dressed and meet me in my office where we can talk some more."

"You're finished with the exam?" he asked.

She nodded. "With the basics. Congratulations." She stepped into the hall and let him walk past her and into the small exam room.

Winter sat on the table wrapped in a blue gown with a paper sheet covering her to her waist. Beside her stood Nikki, looking at him with a huge grin on her face. His baby's mother didn't look nearly as happy to see him.

"Ladies," he greeted them with a smile.

"I think that's my cue to leave!" Nikki gathered her bag and jacket she'd hung on a hook behind the door and walked over to her sister.

She wrapped her arms around Winter and whispered something in her ear, then stepped past him, squeezing his hand in silent support as she left, pulling the door shut behind her.

Harrison glanced around the room, taking in the medical instruments and stirrups on either side of the table, grateful for his timing. He'd missed the exam, and he had a feeling it was for the best this time.

He cleared his throat and met Winter's glassy green eyes. With her makeup-free face and her arms wrapped around herself, holding her gown shut—and probably herself together—she looked more fragile than he'd ever seen her.

"This is why you called me, right? You wanted to

tell me you'd made an appointment?"

She nodded. "I was going to ask if you wanted to come along, but… you were busy."

He inclined his head. "Watching auditions." And the rest they would discuss another time. Right now, he needed to be succinct. "I'm here now, and this is how things are going to be. You. Me. Co-parenting this baby."

She visibly swallowed hard. "I can't—*we* can't—be an obligation."

There was obviously a lot of emotional baggage behind that word, and he'd need to unpack it if they were going to make this work. They had time to do that, but for now, they needed to be in agreement.

"Winter, I don't want to do this the hard way or take extreme measures to be a part of my baby's life. I want to make this work *with* you. Will you let me?"

Her lower lip trembled as she obviously thought about his words. "I want my baby to have what I never did. If you want to be a steady presence, if you aren't going to be someone who pops in and out of my child's life, then okay. We can do this. Together."

Relief washed over him, and he nodded. A part of him wanted to pull her into his arms and promise her everything would be okay, but she was stiff and didn't seem as if she'd be receptive to his comfort. Not when he was the one pushing her.

"How about we go for lunch after the appointment and talk? I have some things I want to explain to you. Things that I hope will make *me* easier for you to understand." Instead of a hug, he took her cold hand in his. "Are you free?"

After a brief hesitation, she nodded. "I am."

"Good. I'll step out so you can get dressed. We'll talk to the doctor and then you can pick your favorite food or restaurant."

"I want mac and cheese."

He couldn't help but grin. "You got it."

Then he needed to set her straight about what had happened in LA.

AFTER HER DOCTOR'S appointment, Winter found herself at Harrison's brother's bar. The Back Door was a small neighborhood pub in the Flatiron District near Union Square in Midtown Manhattan. Harrison had mentioned he called Zach and told him he wanted a back booth and privacy, instructing him to clear out anyone near their table.

She figured it was nice to get what you wanted and needed at any moment in time.

When they walked into the bar, she'd noticed that although the bar decor was old-looking by design with scarred, dark wooden tables and chairs, there was no big screen television on the wall to distract from conversation.

Well, then. She was obviously in for that talk he wanted to have, and she needed to hear what he had to say. She could admit that much.

She still couldn't believe he'd shown up at her appointment and announced his intention to be there for everything involving the baby. If he meant it, her child would have a father in his or her life. Everything Winter had never had. And her baby deserved the world. Especially a father who loved her and she needed to trust Harrison would get there. Eventually.

Settled into the booth, he pushed aside the menus.

A pretty brunette caught his action and walked over to the table. "Hi, Harrison. Good to see you." The woman's gaze slid to Winter, and she smiled. "What can I get you to drink, hon?"

Since she was friendly to Winter, this server wasn't the type of woman Harrison told her about during their interview talks. She wasn't a fan girl who was jealous of Harrison's female companion.

"Winter, this is Raven, Zach's best server. Raven, meet Winter," Harrison said.

She smiled. "Nice to meet you. And I'd love a club soda with lots of ice. In a huge glass. I'm so thirsty."

"Of course," Raven said. "Harrison?"

"Diet Coke. Winter will have mac and cheese." He glanced at her. "Sloppy joes? Roasted broccoli?"

"Both." She laughed as she answered, suddenly very hungry, too.

A relieved expression crossed Harrison's face. "I'll have the same thing."

Raven nodded, scooped up the menus, and walked toward the bar and kitchen.

"Is your brother here?" Winter glanced around, not seeing a familiar face. She'd met Zach a few times but didn't know him well.

Harrison shook his head. "Zach said he had things to do today. I knew Raven would help me out, and they really do have the best mac and cheese. Not to mention all the privacy we need."

She grinned. "I'm not sure if I should say it's good to be famous, or in this case, good to be a Dare." Turning to him, she studied his face.

It wasn't like she hadn't seen him up close before. When he was deep inside her body, she'd looked into those indigo-blue eyes, seen the creases on the sides and the dimple in his cheek before his full lips had come down on hers. In the moment, she hadn't been thinking she was with Harrison Dare, the world-famous actor or hottest playboy. He'd just been the man who affected her more than any other.

But she'd still had every intention of walking away

when their time together was over, but Mother Nature had other ideas. And here they were.

She inhaled, and his scent filled her nostrils. Vanilla and spice, and she couldn't help but lean into him and take a deeper breath.

"We need to talk." The smile now lifting his lips told her she'd been caught smelling him before he sobered, looking serious. "I want to tell you what happened at the audition before you called and saw me covered in lipstick."

She straightened her shoulders and moved back, giving herself space. "It's fine. Honestly. You don't owe me an explanation." Nor did she want to know.

If she was going to survive them being co-parents, she didn't need to hear about his love life. She might not believe in happily ever after, but she couldn't deny jealousy when she felt it. And seeing that lipstick on his face had hurt.

"But I *need* to explain."

"Drinks!" Raven said loudly as if she knew she was interrupting and wanted to announce herself. She placed the glasses on the table in front of them. "Food will be out soon."

Once Raven walked away, Harrison turned back to her. "My ex was at the audition, and she wanted a role. She's a big believer in the casting couch. That's why we broke up in the first place." His hands fisted on the table, turning his knuckles white.

Winter processed his words and came to the only conclusion she could. "She cheated on you to get a movie part?" she asked, horrified.

As a reporter who'd interviewed everyone from actors to popstars, she knew how things worked. She just couldn't believe any sane woman would cheat on Harrison Dare.

"She did." He ground his teeth at the memory. "I haven't seen her in years, but she walked into the room uninvited after her audtion." He shook his head. "It's sad because her audition was great, but no way will I hire her."

Winter studied him. "Why not?"

"First, she tried to convince me she wanted to get back together and when that ploy didn't work, she offered to sleep with me in exchange for the part. She was making the offer and rubbing herself all over me when you called."

Her eyes opened wide. "And that's how you ended up with the lipstick."

He nodded. "When the cell rang, I figured the call was saving me. I had no idea she'd left her imprint behind."

Winter was unable to hold back a sigh, feeling bad for him. "I'm sorry you got caught up in that."

"And I'm sorry you saw it and misinterpreted

things. For good reason, but still."

"So… it wasn't what it looked like." Just as he and Nikki had insisted.

All the tension inside her eased, and she hated that she was relieved he hadn't been sleeping with someone right after learning Winter was having his baby. But she was.

"And here's your meal!" Raven announced. She placed the dishes on the table, and a busboy gave each of them a plate to share the food.

Alone again, Harrison reached for her plate and scooped the delicious-looking mac and cheese onto one. He loaded a soft bun with the sloppy joe beef and sauce next. By the time he added the broccoli, her stomach was rumbling and her mouth was watering.

"I'm glad you're hungry. How has the morning sickness been?" he asked, serving up his own lunch.

"Every day is different. Sick, not sick… right now, I'm fine." And since she was starving, she intended to take advantage.

They ate in silence, Harrison seeming to realize she needed the time to devour her meal, which was in parts cheesy and all comfort food. He did the same.

The lull in conversation gave her time to think, and what she decided was that she needed to trust Harrison. There was nothing in what he said or did that led her to think he wasn't sincere. He'd opened up to her, and she believed him. Her gut, the same one she trusted in her job, had her believing him now. Besides, her baby deserved a father, and she had to admit Harrison had begun to step up. He was trying.

Raven stopped by to refill their drinks and returned to clear the plates, leaving them alone again to talk.

It was her turn. Winter drew a deep breath. "I won't keep you from your child. If you want to be a part of the whole process, I'll keep you informed."

He let out a relieved groan and grinned. She hoped their child inherited that smile and dimple. "That's a good start. Thank you."

After his revelation about his ex, he deserved some honesty, too. "I might not always do things the right way. You have to understand, I didn't grow up with a father. I never had a man in my life I let get close. It was my mom and me, and I have a good relationship with my mentor, Erin Sawyer. But Mom died, and Erin moved to Washington, DC." She shrugged. "I'm used to being alone."

She'd been pushing away that truth because it hurt to think about her mother missing out on being a grandmother, especially when Juliana had been such a wonderful parent.

"I'm sorry you lost her and that she won't be around for the baby," he said, compassion in his gaze.

"Thank you." There was still more that Harrison needed to know about her in order to understand her gut reaction to push people away.

"When I realized I was pregnant, I knew I could do what my mom did with me." She stirred her straw in her drink, pulling her thoughts together. "I'm lucky enough to have the financial means to take care of myself and the baby. All I knew was you'd told me you didn't want a family—"

He held up one hand, and she paused to let him speak.

"Did it ever dawn on you that I have a canned answer ready to go when a reporter asks that question about marriage and family? If I said, yes, I want kids, I'd open myself up to the crazy women out there."

She frowned but realized he had a point, and as a reporter, she should have known better than to jump to conclusions. A journalist should always take an independent perspective. But this was such a personal situation, and she'd blown it. "I'm sorry about that. I wasn't thinking clearly."

"Neither was I," he said wryly. "And you aren't alone. Not anymore. You have Nikki," he reminded her. "And Derek, and once you get to know them, my crazy crew."

She wasn't ready to discuss being overwhelmed by his family, strangers who pulled people into their inner circle easily. Unlike her.

"Nikki and Derek are new to me." But they'd become close quickly because once Winter discovered she had siblings, a need she'd never acknowledged took hold inside her.

"But you took her with you to the doctor's today."

"I needed her to hold my hand," she admitted.

A grin lifted his sexy lips. "I would have held your hand."

She couldn't fight the smile that tugged at her own mouth. "I'm just not used to relying on anyone, and I'm not sure I know how."

Her sister was somehow different. Maybe because she was a part of her. Bound by blood and all that.

"I think we can figure it out. Together."

She managed a nod, surprised at the relief she felt. She didn't feel like she'd lost the fight, more like she'd gained a partner. Just maybe it wouldn't be so bad to have help. *He was here.* Not for her but for the baby, and she needed to remember the distinction when that traitorous warmth rose inside her chest around Harrison.

They finished their meal. After Raven boxed their leftovers, the car ride uptown was quick, and when they reached Winter's building, Harrison climbed out and extended a hand to help her out of the back seat.

"Thank you," she said, expecting him to leave her

at the entrance where the doorman held the door open, waiting for her to walk into the lobby.

To her surprise, Harrison shut the car door, and the Uber drove away without him. She looked up at him, and he shrugged. "I'm walking you to the door. My stepmom raised me to be a gentleman."

She knew from her interview with him that he'd been raised by his father and the woman Michael Dare had married, who happened to be his kids' nanny. There'd been no cheating or naughty business. The couple hadn't gotten together until long after Harrison's biological mom had passed. She'd died by suicide when he was a young boy, and by then, Serenity might as well have been the Dare children's mom.

"Let's go inside." Harrison placed a hand on Winter's back.

Doing her best to ignore the warmth he caused and the tingling between her thighs, she walked into the building. They stepped past the front desk, through the lobby and into the elevators.

A few minutes later, they were at her door, and he propped one shoulder against the wall, his gaze steady on hers. "Will you check in with me? Let me know how you're feeling?"

Surprise flared inside her. That wasn't about the baby. Or was it? "If something's ever wrong, I promise I'll let you know."

His eyes narrowed, and he shook his head. "I don't

just mean check in about the baby." He reached out, brushing his knuckles down her cheek. "I want to know *you're* okay."

That warmth blazed to life inside her again. Then he leaned in and kissed her cheek, his lips cool against her skin. If she turned her face an inch, their mouths would meld, and she was oh so tempted to give in. But nothing had changed. Neither of them wanted a relationship, and she had someone more important to consider now. Harrison was only here with her now because she was carrying his baby.

She stepped back, her heart thudding against her chest.

Hooded eyes looked down at her. "Unlock your door," he said in a gruff voice.

She shook her head to clear it and pulled her keys from her bag.

He took them from her and inserted the metal into the cylinder, then turned the key, opening her door. He stepped back to let her inside.

"Thanks for everything, Harrison. I'll… be in touch."

"And so will I." He treated her to his heartbreaking smile, but she saw the deeper man beneath.

The one who'd been shocked when an unwanted pregnancy had sent him reeling, then pulled himself together and promised to be a father to their unborn baby.

Chapter Six

WINTER WOKE UP feeling slightly queasy, but she pushed through, doing a ten-minute meditation session before getting out of bed, doing her bathroom routine, then walking the dog. The fresh air felt cool against her skin, and she was in a good mood, both from yesterday's doctor's appointment and Harrison's surprising insistence on a partnership of sorts.

Although she was wary, she was also grateful. She might have been willing to go through the experience alone, but she was glad she didn't have to. And her baby would have both his or her parents, which in the end was all that mattered.

Leash in hand, she turned the corner back onto her street, her mind on the cup of tea she'd make herself when she returned to her apartment.

Instead of the empty sidewalk she'd passed when she'd started her walk, a large group of people now congregated by the entrance where her doorman would normally greet her.

She slowed, pulling on Panda's leash to keep her close. "What in the world is going on?" she asked aloud. Before she could decide whether to push her way through the crowd, she heard her name and turned.

A familiar man in a leather jacket walked up to her. "Zach?" She'd met Harrison's brother while spending time in the Hamptons this past summer, but she'd never run into him near her building.

He looked her over, giving her a chance to take in his appearance. His hair was mussed, his lips turned downward in a deep frown. "Come on. I need to get you out of here." He grasped her arm and turned her away from the throng of people toward the way she'd come.

Panda began to bark and she bent down to soothe her before glancing back up at Zach.

"Wait, why?"

"I'll explain on the way." He began to walk and she rushed along with him but didn't understand what was happening.

"The news just broke." He stopped by a black SUV with tinted windows and hit the button on a key fob.

She wrinkled her nose in confusion. "What news?" She patted the phone in her sweatshirt pocket she'd grabbed out of habit. "I woke up, dressed, and went out to walk the dog without looking online or checking my cell. What's going on?"

"Come on. Hop in, and I'll explain." He opened the passenger door, and though she was confused, she trusted Zach.

Scooping Panda into her arms, Winter climbed into the SUV.

Zach strode around the car and joined her, locking the doors and closing them in.

"What's happening? Where's Harrison? Why are you here?" She had so many questions.

He stretched his arm over the back of her seat, turning to meet her gaze. "He's at his apartment. He didn't come himself because he didn't want the vultures to see him at your place. And the reason is that someone alerted the news about your situation."

"What situation?" What was she missing in this conversation?

He swiped the screen on his phone, tapped a few times, and turned his cell to face her. He'd pulled up the Celebrity Gossip Central site for her to see.

Hollywood's Hottest Baby Daddy.

Harrison Dare was spotted in an obstetrician's office on Park Avenue yesterday. A source tells us he was looking for Winter Capwell, the newly revealed illegitimate daughter of ex-Senator Corbin Bettencourt. Stay tuned for more news as it comes in.

"Oh my God." Winter buried her face in Panda's

soft fur. Her entire life had exploded, and she hadn't even known about it.

"That's one way to put it." Zach rubbed her back with his big hand. "Hey, it's going to be okay. Let's get you to Harrison's, and we can come up with a plan."

He picked up his phone and typed out what seemed like a long message before starting the engine and pulling out of the parking spot.

Meanwhile, she sat in her seat, heart pounding hard in her chest. The queasiness had turned into full-fledged nausea, and she did her best to stay calm and hoped it would ease. The car sped through the city, and it wasn't long before they drove past another building with reporters swarming the front entrance, just as they'd done at hers.

"I'm changing professions," she muttered, not wanting anything to do with reporters who ruined people's lives for a living.

Zach let out a chuckle. "There's a difference. You only interview willing people."

He turned the corner and pulled up to a closed garage door, honking so the crowd at this entrance would move aside. They scattered and she could see them attempting to see into the SUV, cameras raised, probably snapping photos.

"Any reason you have tinted windows?" she asked, grateful she was protected but curious anyway.

He shrugged as he pressed a garage door opener on his visor and the massive door opened. "Privacy is important, and as you can see, with a famous brother, it comes in handy."

As soon as the SUV entered the garage, the large doors closed behind them. Zach drove to a parking spot at the far end of the garage near a bank of two elevators.

He angled the vehicle between the two lines and cut the engine. "What was your plan if you hadn't run into me on the street?" she asked Zach.

"Well, you didn't answer your phone, so I planned on having the doorman call upstairs or bribe him to let me up. Whichever worked."

Panda wriggled in her lap, and she opened the door so she could climb out and let the dog down.

Zach hopped out and met her on her side of the vehicle, taking the dog so she could ease out of the car. He placed Panda on the ground, and they walked beside Zach to the elevator.

"This one goes to the penthouse floor," he said, pointing to the left side and scanning his phone screen on a wall sensor.

When the doors slid open, they stepped in, and the elevator took them to the top floor. As the doors reopened, Harrison was waiting in his entryway. He looked her over and visibly relaxed, his shoulders dropping down as he blew out a relieved breath.

"I texted him to alert him we'd arrived," Zach answered her unasked question.

Harrison took three long strides into the private hallway and hauled her into his arms. "I was so fucking worried." His strong arms pulled her against him, and she inhaled his sexy yet somehow comforting scent. He held her for a long beat until Zach cleared his throat and chuckled.

Harrison stepped back and looked her over, obviously checking her out in a concerned way. "Are you okay?"

She nodded. "Zach rescued me when I came home from walking the dog before anyone noticed me."

He shot his brother a grateful look.

"Okay, kids, I'm out of here," Zach said. "Yell if you need me." He reached out and squeezed her hand. "Don't worry. As you know, another story will replace yours soon enough, and you'll be yesterday's news."

She smiled and nodded. "True enough."

"Kids," Harrison muttered, repeating his brother with a shake of his head. "You do remember I'm older than you?"

Grinning, Zach saluted him. "Bye, bro." He tapped the elevator button, which opened immediately. He stepped in, the door closed, and Zach was gone.

Harrison turned to Winter. "Come on in." He

placed a hand on her back and led her inside, locking the door behind them. "Let's sit." He clasped her hand in his and led her to the long, plush sofa they'd had sex on this summer.

She flushed at the memory and lowered herself onto one of the cushions. He joined her, his leg rubbing against hers. He didn't move away, and she admitted to herself that she needed his strength.

"I've never been the subject of a story before. It's so weird to be on the other side." She slid her tongue over her bottom lip. "How in the world did they find out about us and the baby?"

He put his hand on her knee, meeting her gaze, his eyes a deep shade of navy and his expression filled with regret. "I am so sorry. If I had any idea showing up at the appointment yesterday would have led to this, I wouldn't have come." He ran a hand through his hair. "I just wanted to see you, and I didn't think."

She tipped her head to the side and waited for him to continue.

"Someone from the doctor's office leaked the story," he finally said. "Since none of the patients in the waiting room knew who I came to see, I would guess it was one of the staff or a nurse."

Her blood turned hot, her anger a palpable thing. "That's totally unethical, not to mention a HIPAA violation," she said as she reached into her pocket to find her phone.

"Don't. I already gave my lawyers all the necessary information. Believe me when I tell you whoever leaked the news will be out of a job, be brought up before a medical board, and hopefully lose his or her license."

She flopped against the back of the sofa with an angry groan. "Thank you."

She couldn't be upset that he'd taken control because his way would be much more effective than her calling and yelling at whoever answered the phone.

"Winter, I promised to take care of things for you, and I will," he said in a gruff voice.

She narrowed her gaze. "You mean you'll take care of things for the baby."

"I *mean,* for both of you."

A part of her, the one who longed for stability and love, wished he meant it in a way that meant she belonged to him and immediately pushed the thought away. Wanting more from him than he could give was dangerous. He'd make certain she was protected and for that, she was grateful.

Her stomach let out a low, unladylike growl, hunger suddenly gnawing at her insides. A blush hit her cheeks. "I didn't eat breakfast. Come to think of it, neither did Panda." She glanced down at the pup who'd curled at her feet and gone to sleep after the long walk.

"I can make you something to eat. How about eggs?"

She shook her head hard, the thought making her want to gag. She needed something sweet. "I know of a crepe place that delivers." She was suddenly craving a Nutella and banana crepe.

After she pulled up the menu on her cell and showed him the menu, they ordered, and she was ready to deal with reality.

"What am I going to do? I want to go home, shower and change, and I can't." She glanced down at her black checkered flannels. "I'm wearing pajama pants and I have nothing else to put on. Panda needs to eat, and I need to get her food." The list of necessities grew, and she hated that she felt stuck here. "What if I go home after we eat, and I'll ignore the paparazzi as I go inside."

Harrison shook his head. "More like they will push and shove one another to get to you, and you could get hurt. I won't let that happen. But I did think ahead. Zach texted after he picked you up and he told me you'd need a change of clothing. Nikki will be here soon with some clothes and toiletries. I'll just call her and add dog food to the list." He lifted the phone already in his hand.

"Wait. Toiletries?" she asked, confused.

He met her gaze. "You're going to have to stay here for a night or two until the news cycle picks up another story." His thinned lips told her he was serious.

"We can't go home?"

He reached out and covered her hand with his. "Even if we managed to get you inside your building, you'd be stuck in your apartment until the paps leave."

She blinked, thinking about what that meant. "But I need to be able to walk Panda."

"And you'd be alone. Not ideal for dog walking. The bodyguard firm I use said they'd send someone to help us out. I could have them cover you at your place, but to be honest, I'd feel better if you stayed here until the news isn't as exciting." He smiled, showing her his dimple. As if he knew the grin would help his cause and she wouldn't be able to resist his request.

She groaned because she absolutely couldn't. Not when her, her baby's, and her beloved dog's safety and security were at stake.

"I can cook. Added incentive, obviously." He waggled his eyebrows, and she dipped her head and laughed.

"You're incorrigible. But you're right. It was insane outside, both there and here. And I can't be stuck alone."

Besides, she couldn't deny staying here would

make her feel safer. Calmer. Oh, screw it. She just wanted to be here until things blew over. No excuses needed. She was sure he had a guest room, or he wouldn't have made the offer.

"Okay," she said. "Thank you. I'll stay."

His eyes warmed and he nodded. "I'll call Asher and ask them to pick up dog food." He turned over his phone, slid his finger over the screen, and made a call. He spoke to Asher and hung up before turning to face her.

"Do you always take control like this? Does Zach?" She already knew Asher was the same way, and she didn't know what to make of these Dare men who were so in charge.

"I am, and there are reasons." He drew in a deep breath and let it out slowly. "My mom left when I was six. She couldn't handle being a mother, but she loved being pregnant." He shook his head and let out a sigh. "I won't pretend to understand her psyche, but I know she was mentally ill. I try not to blame her, but the fact is, Serenity was more of a mother to me than my biological parent."

A lump rose to Winter's throat and settled there. Unable to listen to his story without touching him, she reached for his hand and curled her fingers around his. "I'm sorry. I know she passed away."

He nodded. "Died by suicide. We already had Serenity, but even with a nanny, there were still five kids. Nick and Jade were only two at the time. Eventually, they had the triplets, then five years later, Layla was born—she was an oops baby too," he said with an endearing grin.

Winter smiled at the revelation. "I guess they'll understand about us then."

"Oh, they already do and they're excited. And looking forward to meeting you."

She didn't reply to that. Instead, she placed her hand on her belly protectively. "So then what happened?" she asked him.

"Well, eventually, Dad hired Maggie, our housekeeper, but not for years, so we all grew up quickly. I helped around the house, and I learned to cook. As the oldest, Asher stepped up, taking on the role of herding us all when Dad was at work."

"I had no idea how complicated your childhood was," she murmured. Not even after interviewing him and writing what she thought was an in-depth piece on him and his partners.

Given what she was now learning about Harrison and his family, she realized he'd only revealed superficial information to her in her interview.

So much for being a crack reporter, she thought wryly. "And to think, I spent a month with you." She heard the accusation in her tone. "Why did you hold all this back?"

He shrugged. "I told you the facts you could read anywhere. The rest? I didn't want to tell Winter, the reporter." He cleared his throat. "I'm more comfortable admitting things to Winter, the woman." His voice turned gruff, and her traitorous body responded to both his words and his deep tone.

And when he turned their clasped hands over and drew circles on her skin, awareness oozed through her veins like liquid desire. But the need he inspired didn't stop her mind from working. Harrison Dare was very good at hiding the important parts of himself. He was an actor, and she'd do well to remember that.

Still… "I'm glad you're confiding in me. I like getting to know you. It will make co-parenting easier. And there's no reason to tell me the things you say tonight are *off the record*," she said wryly.

He chuckled. "I know that, or I wouldn't have been honest. I trust you, Winter. I did this summer, too. But I didn't want personal information out there for public consumption. There are things even a celebrity needs to keep private."

Something she understood even better now that her biggest secret had been shared with the world. "I get it." The conversation had her thinking of her sister. "I only thought I understood when naked photos of Nikki were taken and posted on the internet but now I really understand how utterly violated she must have felt."

He nodded. "Being in the public eye sucks sometimes."

And now she'd be raising a child of someone the press would constantly go after. Just one more thing to worry about. But at least she'd have Harrison's help with protecting their child.

Suddenly she remembered the senator and how this might affect him.

"Harrison... the senator."

"What about him?" Harrison asked.

She swallowed hard. "He was named in that article about us. I was so frazzled I forgot to check in with him. I'm sure the press is all over him, too." And though she didn't owe him anything, how could she not feel bad that her personal situation had probably added to the man's already shaky public image?

Harrison's phone buzzed, and he glanced at the table where the screen flashed. "It's a message from *my* father," Harrison said.

She pointed to the phone. "Why don't you talk to him, and I'll call my... father." Calling anyone that still sounded so strange to her ears.

He braced his hands on her shoulders. "Remember something, okay?"

His gorgeous eyes met hers. "What?"

"We're in this together," he said.

He really liked that word, she mused. Unfortunately, *she* liked it too. A little too much.

AFTER HANGING UP with his dad and stepmom, Harrison heard Winter's voice coming from the family room. She was obviously still on the phone with her biological father. Giving her privacy, Harrison remained in his room and walked to the window, looking at the sun-filled sky and the cityscape below. The view was one of the reasons he'd chosen this building and looking out at the city gave him peace. Not as much as the ocean at the Hamptons home he'd purchased when he realized his siblings were going to spend more of their time out east than here in Manhattan. And K-Talent's main offices were here, too.

Winter's voice traveled to him again, and he hoped she was getting as much support from her parent as Harrison received from his family. Given the little Nikki and Derek had gotten growing up, Harrison was concerned, but at least the senator was trying to build a relationship with his daughter.

Since both Michael and Serenity already knew about Winter's pregnancy, their call had been about today's headlines. They already knew how crazy

Harrison's life could get, and Zach had filled them in about the reporters crowding the entrances to his and Winter's buildings. His parents had invited Harrison and Winter to stay at their house, something he knew Winter would never go for.

Harrison was just learning how deep her trust issues ran and why. The daughter of a single mom who'd hammered home the notion of being independent and not needing a man to get by? Yeah, Harrison was lucky she was being more open with the notion of letting him into her pre-baby pregnancy life. Especially since she'd just discovered how difficult being involved with his celebrity status could be. It was too soon to surround her with his overly large family.

He thought back to their conversation earlier. He'd never expected to discuss his mother's suicide and how he'd grown up feeling like he needed to control things around him. But Winter was easy to talk to, and he didn't mean the reporter who put on a smile and had a pushy persona. He'd opened up to the woman herself.

She'd listened, had a good sense of humor, was compassionate... and she was having his baby.

He liked *her*.

He was attracted to both her gorgeous face and the curves he'd memorized with his hands and mouth. He was drawn to her intelligence. When they'd hooked up this summer, they'd been in agreement. Neither had been looking for a relationship. He wasn't sure he felt the same way now.

He needed to know more about Winter, to understand her, and maybe even get back into her bed. Because Harrison had a feeling the more time they spent together, the more he would want from her. From the day they'd met, he hadn't been able to get her out of his head. He didn't see that changing any time soon.

Going back to LA and seeing his ex had reminded him how much he hated the shallow life he'd tried to leave behind. He already realized how much he'd screwed up when he heard the news that he was going to be a father. Then he'd had hours on a plane to think and come to the conclusion that he might just be ready for what his brothers and sister had.

Which surprised him. He'd been living in New York for a couple of years and watching his siblings find the one person who completed them. He'd told himself he didn't need or want the same thing because he hadn't thought he could trust a woman to desire him for the man he was, not the famous face, the huge career, and the money he had.

Then Winter showed up, and she'd gotten to him. For the first time in his life, he hadn't minded a woman digging in deep. She, however, wanted to do it all on her own. It was ironic. The one woman he might see a future with was the one who wasn't pushing him for more.

"Harrison?"

He spun around at the sound of her voice. Winter stood in the doorway, hand raised, ready to knock if he didn't acknowledge her.

"Hey. You spoke to your... to the senator?" He used the title because once a senator, always a senator, and she seemed more comfortable speaking that way about the man, at least for now.

"Everything okay?" he asked.

She nodded, moving closer to him. "He saw the headlines. I've been avoiding meeting up with him, but he wants to talk. I said I'd come to his hotel today. There's no way we can meet in public given all the scandals I've somehow caused." Her cheeks flushed an adorable pink.

"You didn't cause a thing. But I understand what you mean. Do you mind if I ask you a question?"

"Go ahead."

"Why haven't you met with him before now?"

She gave him a forced smile. "Nikki asked me the same question, and the answer is easy. I don't like how hurt Nikki is from how her parents treated her. I know they turned away from her in a hotel lobby in front of donors. How do I form a relationship with the man if

I love my sister?"

Harrison understood. "I'm certain he followed his wife's lead, which is no excuse. And Derek has told me all about how awful his mother was to Jessica, his fiancée. But Corbin Bettencourt left his wife and gave up his seat on the United States Senate when he found out what she'd done. When he found out about you."

Winter opened her mouth to interrupt, and he held up a hand.

"Bear with me, okay? I'm just saying that it's fine to give him a chance to explain, at the very least. One day, maybe Nikki will do the same. Maybe not. Is she pressuring you to not meet with him?"

Winter shook her head. "Just the opposite. She wants me to form my own opinion, but she's hurt that he's trying so hard with me." She pulled her lush lower lip into her mouth and released it again.

He shook his head, ignoring the pulse in his dick because now was not the time.

"To be fair," Winter continued. "He's trying with Nikki, too. She's just not ready to hear it. Derek cuts him more slack because they had a closer relationship to begin with." She shrugged. "Anyway, given the circumstances, I agreed to meet him today."

"The bodyguard from Alpha Security will be here soon." Harrison's entire family utilized the firm, including Dash Kingston. "Whoever shows up will go with you." Though he hated sending her alone. Not that he didn't think she could handle it, but everyone needed support.

Her fingers clenched and released, a sure sign of the tension she was feeling.

"Actually, I was wondering if you'd come with me?" She glanced at him with gorgeous emerald eyes that glistened with unshed tears. "For all my independent talk, I'm stressed about meeting with the man whose life I all but destroyed."

He brushed a hand down her cheek. "I need to repeat, the implosion of his life is not on you. His wife... or soon-to-be ex-wife, was at fault. So was he."

For having the affair with her mother in the first place. For letting his wife run roughshod over him and control not just his career but his relationship with his existing children. And he hated to hear Winter keep blaming herself.

"Of course, I'll come." The protective part of his nature that came out around Winter was glad she wanted him there.

Gratitude shone in her eyes. "Thank you, Harrison."

He liked how his name sounded coming from those lips.

She stepped forward, and he thought for sure she would hug him, but his doorbell rang, the dog began barking, and a voice called out. "Hello! Where is everyone?"

"Nikki," they both said at the same time, Winter taking a step back.

"Asher's on my list of people the doorman can let up without calling, and he has a key," Harrison muttered, annoyed because his brother had cockblocked him.

If Winter had stepped into his personal space and wrapped her arms around him, no matter her reason, he'd have pulled her in for a long, drawn-out kiss. The desire to taste her was always there and growing stronger with every hour they spent together.

They walked out of the bedroom and down the hall to the main area of the apartment where his brother and his fiancée waited, a ton of bags surrounding them. Nikki had brought clothes for Winter, and as requested, they'd stopped to buy dog food, bowls and other things from a pet store.

"Harrison, can you show me the guest room? I want to take a quick shower and clean up before I... have my meeting." Obviously Winter wanted to talk to Nikki in private about her upcoming meeting with their father.

"Guestroom?" Nikki asked, obviously surprised because she knew how many bedrooms his apartment had and about the gym and office space he used them for.

Harrison winced. He hadn't explained details when he'd asked Winter to stay.

Asher wrapped an arm around Nikki and hauled her against him. "Hush," he said to his fiancée as he smirked at Harrison.

Winter narrowed her gaze. "What's going on?"

He ran a hand through his hair and sucked it up. "I don't exactly have a guest room. This place has three bedrooms. One's the primary, one's a workout room, and the other is my office." He tried his grin on her again but this time she didn't bite.

"But I assumed that's where I'd sleep." She shook her head and sighed. "Never mind, and don't say it. I know what happens when people *assume*." Stepping over to him, she shoved her arm against his shoulder. "Where did you think I'd stay?"

He shrugged, well aware they had an audience. "My California King is pretty big."

She threw up her hands and groaned. "I don't have time for an argument, but we will discuss this later."

"I'm looking forward to it," he muttered, and she glared at him. "The primary bath has everything you'll need, towels, etc." He gestured with his hand, but she knew where the room was located.

Nikki looked at him and wagged a finger. "Shame, Harrison. Shame." Laughing, she helped Winter pick up all the bags with the clothes and toiletry items she'd brought. "I'll go with Winter."

"Why don't you make yourself useful and feed the dog," his *houseguest* suggested and strode off, not giving him another glance.

Panda, who'd gone from jumping on everyone's legs and nudging their calves with her nose, was now shoving her snout into a bag that probably had the dog food in it.

"Good going." Asher chuckled and picked up the bag with the kibble. "Come on. I'm used to feeding a dog."

"Right. Nikki suckered you into bringing one home from the Bahamas," Harrison said.

"I wouldn't laugh if I were you. Something tells me you're going to be whipped and doing a six a.m. walk right along with me."

Harrison rolled his eyes, but he didn't meet Asher's gaze. Because he had a feeling his brother wasn't wrong.

A little while later, Morgan, their bodyguard, had arrived and checked in. While waiting, he took Panda for a walk, understanding that Harrison couldn't do it himself, and Harrison and Asher talked until the women returned.

Nikki's eyes were red-rimmed, and though Winter had put on makeup for her meeting with her father,

her eyes were bloodshot. It was obvious their talk had been rough on her too.

He and Asher exchanged worried glances.

"We're fine," Nikki said, and Winter nodded in agreement.

"We are."

Asher glanced at his fiancée. "Come on. Let's go home and talk."

After saying their goodbyes, Asher and Nikki left.

Harrison looked at Winter's pale features and resolved to take care of her through this whole mess. "Ready?" He extended his arm.

She slipped her smaller hand into his and their palms pressed together. He curled his fingers around her hand, and they walked out the door to join their security guard and go meet with the senator.

Chapter Seven

SENATORS WEREN'T GIVEN secret service or bodyguard protection, and even if they had been, Corbin Bettencourt was no longer a government official. Ironically, Winter and Harrison had their own security. Morgan drove them out of the building from the garage in a discreet SUV with tinted windows. He parked the vehicle in the hotel garage himself and led them to the bank of elevator doors, glaring at anyone who tried to get close or in the elevator with them.

The senator had given Winter his hotel suite number, and they traveled directly to his floor, her stomach in knots. Her nerves made no sense. She was a reporter. She'd interviewed everyone from sweet human beings to total assholes. So why, as she knocked on the hotel room door, was she so damned anxious?

Harrison kept her hand in his, and he squeezed her fingers. "It's going to be fine, and we can leave whenever you want."

She nodded, grateful for his support. "I can handle this. But I appreciate that you're here with me."

He winked her way just as the door opened and the man who called himself her father stood in the doorway. They stared at each other, Winter taking in familiar features she hadn't realized she shared. Green eyes, the same slightly upturned nose, and similar smile.

"Winter, thank you for coming. I didn't realize you were bringing company."

The senator glanced at Harrison and held out a hand in what seemed like an automatic gesture courtesy of his political days. But he wore a casual pair of slacks and a button-down shirt, and unlike every photograph she'd seen of him, he wasn't wearing a tie, and his sleeves were rolled to his forearms.

It had only been a little while since he'd resigned, but she wondered if he missed his position as someone important in the world.

Harrison reached out and shook the older man's hand.

"Harrison Dare, it's good to meet you," Corbin said, then stepped back and opened the door for them to enter.

Placing a gentle hand on her back, a gesture she was coming to enjoy, Harrison walked into the large suite along with her. Following the senator's lead, they settled onto the sofa, the senator in a chair across from them.

"Can I pour you some coffee?" he asked, gesturing to the carafe and muffins on the glass cocktail table.

Her stomach wasn't just in knots, the often-present, low-level nausea remained. "No, thank you," she said.

Harrison shook his head, too.

"Well. I appreciate you coming," the man she wasn't prepared to call her father or *dad* said.

She clasped her hands on top of her thighs. "I thought it was time we talked."

"I'm glad. I read that congratulations are in order for you both."

Her hand came to her stomach. "Thank you."

"So it's true then?" he asked.

Harrison stiffened. "Was that a test of some sort?" he asked, defensive on her behalf.

Why she found his protectiveness sexy, she had no idea. But she liked the fact that he was looking out for her and not just the baby they would share.

The senator shook his head, holding up his hands, palms out. "Of course not. I'm just aware that you can't believe everything you see or read in the media, and I wanted to hear it from you."

Winter sighed, and Harrison inclined his head. "We both know that's true," he agreed. "So why did you want to see Winter today?"

She stared at the biological parent she didn't understand at all. "Yes, why now?" she asked him. "I know you've been wanting to talk, and I've been putting you off." She could admit to that. "But you did seem more insistent this morning."

The senator crossed an ankle over his thigh, more relaxed than she thought he would be. "Because I was almost certain the news outlets were telling the truth. And if you were pregnant, I thought it was time you understood what happened between me and your mother."

Winter blew out a long breath and her insides trembled, making her glad she hadn't asked for caffeine. "She wouldn't talk about you. In fact, Mom lied for most of my life. She told me she didn't know who my father was." Until the end, but she didn't want to think about her mom being gone, and she needed to hear his story.

As if sensing she needed his strength, Harrison put an arm around her waist and pulled her close.

The senator winced, obviously hurt by the news of her mom not naming him as her father. Which surprised her. "That bothers you?" she asked.

His gaze bore steadily into hers. "You have to trust me when I say I did not know about you."

She swallowed hard. Oddly enough, she believed him.

"If I had known, I'd have come for you. I would have made certain you had a father."

That statement she had an issue with, and she

shook her head in denial. "Like Nikki had a father?"

She didn't mention Derek because he and his father had had a different relationship. Probably because he was the senator's *son*.

"I deserved that." The senator glanced down, but she caught the embarrassed flush on his cheeks. "I made many mistakes with my children. When they were younger, I tried harder to counter my wife's... *icier* tendencies."

"Icy. *That's* what you'd call her? I wasn't there to see her behavior with Nikki firsthand but the day I showed up at your home and told you who I was? She lost her mind." Winter cringed at the memory of Collette, the normally haughty woman Winter had seen on television, shrieking and yelling, when she discovered Winter's mother had kept her child.

She'd called Winter's mother a whore and swore Nikki wouldn't ruin her family. As if the woman hadn't done that on her own.

"I'd never seen her... unhinged like that before. As for myself, she was a hard woman and I admit it became easier not to fight with her and let her dictate how things went."

"That's weak," Winter said, not holding her punches.

He inclined his head. "I agree and I'm trying to change my relationship with both Nicolette and

Derek. I'm not certain it will work." He sighed and Winter understood.

Nikki wasn't budging on forgiving him. Not yet.

"You could start by calling her Nikki," Winter suggested. "Nicolette reminds her of her mother's demands." She didn't think her sister would mind her revealing that bit of truth and Winter wanted Nikki to mend fences if she desired it. Why not make it easier on them?

"I appreciate that." He leaned over, picked up the carafe and poured himself a cup of coffee, adding a dollop of cream. After taking a long sip, he placed the cup down on its saucer.

"Now, about us. There are things I want you to know."

Unable to deny her curiosity, Winter leaned forward, and her knees hit the edge of the glass table. She scooted back. "What are they?" she asked.

The senator rubbed his hands on his navy slacks, obviously deep in thought, before he raised his head and met her gaze. "Your mother was the love of my life."

Stunned, she sucked in a breath, the words hard to hear and even more difficult to believe. "Then why didn't you go after her? I know she disappeared, but you had resources. You could have looked for her."

It was something that had bothered Winter for the

last year that her mother had been gone. No matter what her *father* did or didn't know about Juliana's pregnancy, how much could he have cared for her if he'd let her go so easily.

Another sip of his coffee, then he said, "I received a note from your mother—well at the time I thought it was from her—asking me not to search. She said she'd listened when I'd talked about my future plans for the country, and she couldn't be the reason I didn't have the opportunity to try and change the world." He dipped his head. "I realize how pompous that sounds now."

Oh, it did, Winter thought and narrowed her gaze. "I take it she hadn't written the letter?"

Or maybe she had. If she was leaving the father of her child behind with the money Collette had given her, she'd had to make sure he didn't look for her.

"Collette wrote it. She admitted as much," he said.

Winter nodded and wondered if her mother had left but hoped the *love of her life* would come searching for her only to be disappointed.

"So you chose your career over the woman you claimed to love," she said, not cutting him any slack.

"I suppose I did." He ran a hand through his salt and pepper hair. "Juliana made it easy by leaving, and once she was gone, Collette took over. I was busy twenty-four-seven with political events and fundraising."

"Nikki said she's manipulative and good at it," Winter muttered.

Beside her, Harrison obviously decided to join the senator and poured himself coffee. "Want some?" he asked her.

She shook her head. "No, thanks." She was jittery enough.

The senator started to speak again. "I realize now Collette kept me busy, so I wouldn't have time to think about Juliana." He shook his head. "And I admit there was a part of me that was ambitious enough to push thoughts of your mother away and concentrate on our political plans. And then Collette got pregnant with Nikki."

Finally, Winter understood. "After your wife found out about your affair, she got herself pregnant. How did she find out about you and Mom?"

Her mother hadn't had any idea how Collette knew about them, let alone that Juliana was pregnant. The one and only conversation her mother had had with Corbin's wife was the day Collette brought her the check and told her to get rid of *that baby*.

Even now, the thought had bile churning in her gut. How had Nikki and Derek come from that woman? Did their goodness come from their father? *Her* father?

"Apparently, my wife didn't trust me." His lips twisted in a self-deprecating frown. "She wasn't wrong not to. After you showed up at the house and I found out I had another daughter, Collette admitted she'd had me followed and knew I was meeting up with a woman. She'd then had Juliana followed as well." He placed his cup on the table and sighed. "Collette came from money, you see. Whatever she wanted, she was able to have. In me, I'm afraid she saw a man she could mold and do her bidding."

"Your wife was a piece of work." As was he, since he'd let her manipulate him. Winter shook her head, disappointed in him despite already knowing the truth.

"I can't argue with that. But Collette and the political world, that life is behind me. No matter what you or my other children think of me, I am trying to change. And the reason I wanted to talk to you today is to apologize. I'm sorry you grew up without a father. I'm sorry Nikki would have been better off with parents other than the ones she had. I should have done better. I will do better. If you let me."

Throughout his speech of sorts, a lump rose in the back of Winter's throat. While growing up with a mother who'd adored her, she'd told herself she didn't need a father. Hadn't wanted one. Hadn't missed having one. Her mother had hammered home the need for independence, and she'd taken those words

119

to heart.

But now, face to face with the parent she'd never had, Winter considered the possibility that she'd been lying to herself. Telling herself her life was fine without a dad because she had no choice.

Now she did.

"Would you tell me about your mom?" he asked, sounding eager for any information about the woman he said he'd loved. "About *your* life? And what Juliana ultimately did tell you about me?" the senator asked, his voice choked up.

Winter swallowed hard. The day she'd revealed herself to him, she'd informed him that her mother had passed away, but she hadn't gone into detail. Exposing his wife's role in paying off her mother and insisting Juliana have an abortion had been more important.

Today, though, she decided it was time. Harrison sat silently by her side as she detailed her childhood in Maine. Her mom had gotten a new job as a legal secretary, and they'd been happy. They talked about her mom's cancer and the revelation that Senator Corbin Bettencourt was her father.

Before she knew it, the entire afternoon had passed, and then they were standing by the door to the suite and saying their goodbyes.

"I'm glad you came today, and I'll leave it to you to

get back in touch when you're ready," the senator said.

She nodded, appreciating his innate understanding that she needed time to process today. "I'm glad I came, too."

The senator kept a respectful distance, not trying to hug her or push past the emotional boundaries she kept between them.

"Take care, Winter. Thank you for coming, Harrison. I'm sure it was a long day for you."

Winter had thought the same thing. Harrison had sat beside her and listened, not getting involved with their get-to-know-you session.

Harrison shook his head. "It's all good."

Winter looked at the man who was her father, not comfortable using his first name, calling him senator, and especially not saying *dad*. "Goodbye," she murmured as she and Harrison stepped into the hall.

The door shut behind them and there was Morgan, waiting to escort them back to Harrison's apartment. During the course of the afternoon, she'd forgotten about the drama waiting for her outside that large suite.

"Come on. Let's get you two out of here," the large man in a sports jacket said.

Harrison clasped Winter's hand, and they strode down the hall. At her request, Morgan drove by her apartment building. Paparazzi were still outside with cameras and cell phones.

So much for the possibility of her going home. She ought to be upset her life was in utter disarray, yet she couldn't bring herself to be upset she had to stay with Harrison.

HARRISON AND WINTER returned to his apartment, leaving the bodyguard outside. Harrison was used to the occasional need for security, but Winter was not. When the man insisted on walking Panda again, she'd waited for them with soda and a granola bar from the kitchen. She was good to people she didn't know, especially those who went out of their way for her, job or not, reminding Harrison of the women in his family.

Although he had precooked meals in his freezer, courtesy of a private chef who delivered healthy food for people who could afford her crazy prices, he was in the mood for take-out. "Pizza or Chinese?" he asked Winter. "Or if you're nauseous I can make you tea, toast, and jelly."

Her lips quirked up. "Look at you, taking care of your baby mama."

She did that often, he realized, referring back to something about her pregnancy or the baby instead of letting herself think he was being kind to *her*, in order to put emotional distance between them.

"I'll have pizza," she said. "Mushroom, onion, and meatball."

"Nice combo." He wasn't so sure.

She patted her flat stomach. "I'm eating for two. Now, I'm going to change. I want to get more comfortable. I hope Nikki brought me something to sleep in."

"You can grab a tee from my dresser." He thought of Winter in his shirt, her full breasts rubbing against the soft cotton, her nipples poking at the fabric, and he stifled a groan.

She treated him to a small smile. "Thanks. I'll be back."

As she strode toward the primary bedroom, he thought back to his private talk with the senator. Winter had excused herself to use the bathroom, leaving the men alone and her father had jumped on the opportunity to act like the parent he had no right to be. At least not yet.

"Are you two a couple?" he'd asked.

Harrison had stiffened. "That's none of your business," he muttered because he'd have had to say no. And the truth was, he was starting to think he wanted them to be together.

The other man dipped his head, silently acknowledging Harrison's words. *For a one-time senator, he cowed easily*, Harrison thought with a frown.

"I understand," her father said. "Then consider this a word of advice from a man who knew and loved her mother."

Harrison bit his cheek to keep his sarcastic comment inside and waited for the older man to continue.

"If you want to be with Winter, you need to know where she came from." The conversation had happened after her father had told her about her mother being the love of his life. "Juliana was the most independent woman I'd ever met. While my wife needed to mold and guide me, Juliana liked to be her own person, not an extension of a man or a politician."

He paused, letting his words settle, and Harrison listened and digested every word.

"And that was the Juliana I knew *before* she'd had to raise a child alone. I can't imagine how those harder years reinforced her independent beliefs. Or what she taught her daughter."

Harrison had already seen Winter's walls in action when she'd informed him she was pregnant and ready to handle things alone. And each time she reminded them both of the baby—the reason he'd come back to her to begin with.

The creaking of the bathroom door opening had

sounded in the outer room and the senator leaned forward, speaking in a low voice. "All I'm saying is if you want my daughter—and make no mistake, one day she will acknowledge that she is my child—don't give up on her like I did to her mother. And ultimately Winter."

Harrison inclined his head, letting the man know he understood. Corbin Bettencourt hadn't told him anything he hadn't already inferred about Winter but now he had a better understanding of why she was that way.

A while later, they'd eaten dinner, cleaned up, and watched television. Then they'd gone to the bedroom and taken turns in the bathroom. He'd let her go first and once she stepped out, he swallowed a groan.

She was still wearing the soft, white T-shirt she'd taken from him. When she'd walked out of the bedroom earlier, ready for dinner, she'd showered. Her damp hair brushed her shoulders, and her face was shiny from what he assumed was moisturizer. She'd sat down beside him, smelling warm and delicious. Her sister had obviously stocked her up with supplies. Even if Winter was just here for the night, Nikki had taken care of her.

Now, Harrison forced his gaze off Winter's nipples, pert and tight behind the thin tee, as he changed places with her in the bathroom. The room still smelled like her shampoo and body wash. He knew she'd used both, because the pretty bottles sat inside his luxury shower, made with teak floors, marble walls, and a matching wood double vanity. The cream paint added to the neutral tones of the bathroom.

He turned on the hot water and stepped under the spray. He tipped up his head and washed his face, then poured shampoo into his hand. After soaping up his hair, he rinsed and grabbed another bottle, pouring some body wash into his palm.

As he washed, he closed his eyes. A vision of Winter flashed before him. She was kneeling on the floor, her hand around the base of his cock, her mouth sucking him deep. He groaned and when he opened his lids, his slippery hand was pumping his dick, the soap making it easier to milk himself. Arousal rushed through him, and a flash of heat came quickly, telling him he wouldn't last long.

In his mind, Winter's tongue licked his cock, her lips tight around the shaft as he plunged into her wet mouth over and over again. A tingle started low in his spine. His balls drew up and before he knew it, his climax hit and he let out a stifled groan, his come coating the shower floor before the water rinsed it away.

He hoped that orgasm would allow him to climb into bed with her and not get hard as a rock, though he doubted it. Shutting the shower off, he stepped out, picked a towel off the warmer and dried himself off. He finished up his nightly routine, drew a deep breath and walked out to join her, wearing a pair of sweats because... just because he didn't want to freak her out right now.

She'd slid beneath the comforter and sat up against a couple of pillows. She patted the space on his side of the large bed. "Come."

He almost told her he just had. He flipped down the covers, slipping in beside her.

She immediately turned to him. "I wanted to tell you something. I am *so* sorry you had to endure such a long day. I had no idea my—the senator and I would talk for so long. I should have just sucked it up and gone alone." She looked at him through her dark lashes. "But I'm glad I didn't. Thank you."

"You're welcome. I was happy to support you." She'd had time since being with her father to process her feelings. "So what did you think of the man?" Harrison asked.

She blinked and remained silent, obviously weighing her answer. "It was... an emotional afternoon." She slid her tongue over her lush bottom lip. "I was interested in everything he had to say. But... how do I say this? I guess I'm still torn."

He tipped his head to one side. "Why?"

She twisted her hands together, something she did when she was nervous or upset. "I'm trying to decide whether or not I can trust him," she admitted. "Remember, this is the man who ignored his daughter in public and allowed his wife to handle his children in a way that caused emotional damage."

Harrison had heard the story from Asher. Nikki had been devastated when her parents, strolling through the hotel with donors, had seen her and deliberately walked away, ignoring her. It was too risky for them to acknowledge her in public while she was embroiled in her scandal. It had been the last straw, leading to Nikki breaking off any relationship with her mother. Had her father been collateral damage? Time would tell, not only if Asher's fiancée forgave the senator but whether or not he deserved her forgiveness.

"He allowed her mother to belittle and demean her in every way," Winter went on.

She was clearly adding up the reasons not to have a relationship with the man, but Harrison thought she should get to know the man better before making a firm decision. *She needed to give the idea of having her father in her life a chance, if only to understand what her own child needed*, he thought.

He turned to her, reaching out and stroking a hand down her cheek. He'd meant to offer comfort but for

128

him, the touch turned sexual and went straight to his dick.

He shook off that thought. She'd just admitted to having an emotional day. He couldn't prey on her weakened state tonight. They needed to build... or start to build a more solid foundation before he pushed for more. It was a damned good thing Winter couldn't see his hard cock beneath the comforter. Jerking off in the shower hadn't done a damned thing. All he'd had to do was look at Winter and he wanted her.

He forced himself to focus on her life. Her needs. "The senator, *your father*, is also the man who gave up his senate seat after he found out about you and what his wife had done," he reminded her again. "And he's committed himself to fixing things with his children. Shouldn't that mean something?"

She let out a sigh and nodded. "I suppose it does. Do you believe my mother was the love of his life?"

He saw the hope glimmering in her eyes. "I do," he said truthfully. "I think he has a lot of regrets he has to live with." Harrison wanted to change the subject so she could fall asleep on a more positive note.

He thought back to their afternoon and the stories he'd heard about the places the senator had met up with Winter's mom. How they'd kept their affair a secret but enjoyed one another and their time together.

"I liked the stories the senator had about your mother and the ones you told him about your childhood," Harrison said. He appreciated learning about the inquisitive girl she'd been. He understood how she'd ended up becoming a reporter.

"Me too." A warm smile lifted her lips. She studied him for a long beat. "My mother would have liked you, Harrison Dare."

"I'm glad. The question is, do *you*?" The query came out, taking him by surprise.

"Of course I do," she said, her voice thick with real emotion, no walls or barriers to be found.

It was enough for tonight.

"Good." Harrison turned, reached over and flicked off the lamp on the nightstand. "We should get some sleep. Tomorrow we're going to do our best to get you back into your apartment. Even if you decide there are too many reporters and you want to come back here, you can grab some more of your own things."

They each settled beneath the covers, and he heard the sweet sound of her breathing and the small sigh that escaped her lips as she flipped the pillow.

He was awake when her breathing evened out and she fell asleep while he lay beside her, aroused by the thought of her in his bed.

After some time passed, he braced one arm behind

his head and his thoughts turned to the baby. Would he be a good father? He'd had a solid example in both Michael and Asher, who'd stepped up after their mother walked away. Now that the shock had worn off, he wanted nothing more than to be present and there. For both of them.

Chapter Eight

A WET TONGUE licked her face and Winter woke to her dog informing her she wanted to go out. She slipped out of bed, went to the bathroom and dressed, then headed out, leaving Harrison asleep. No sooner had she opened the apartment door than the bodyguard, a different one than the night before, greeted her.

"I'm Ava Talbott. I'm on the day shift today." The attractive woman extended her hand and Winter shook it.

"I'm Winter Capwell, but I'm assuming you know that." She laughed and Ava nodded.

"Does the dog need a walk?" she asked.

Winter nodded. "I'll take her down and stay by the building."

Ava shook her head. "It's part of the job." She took the leash from her. "Don't worry though. I'll stay close and keep an eye on whoever comes in and out while she does her business. And I have the key, so I'll let her inside when I get back."

Okay then. She supposed this was how the other half lived. Bodyguards who walked her dogs. "Thank you. Can I get you something to eat or drink? I have soda, water, juice…"

Ava treated her to a warm smile "No, thank you. I'm good." She glanced at Panda. "Let's go," she said to the pup in an authoritative voice that Winter's dog responded to.

Winter stepped back into the apartment and shut the door.

Knowing Panda would expect food after her morning walk, she headed to the kitchen, measured out kibble and poured the food into a bowl. After placing it beside the water, she walked back to the bedroom and shut the door behind her. Panda had her dog bed in the family room and though she'd slept in Harrison's bed, something she was grateful he hadn't minded, the dog would be fine in the outer area of the apartment after she ate. She was lucky that her pup stuck to a routine.

Once back in the bedroom, her gaze fell to Harrison, asleep in his bed. The covers had dropped low, revealing his tanned chest. He had one arm over his head as he lay on his back, lips slightly parted. *The man oozed sex appeal*, she thought, as she slid beneath the covers on her chosen side.

Of all the scenarios she'd imagined for her life, getting pregnant by a man she'd agreed to have an affair with hadn't been on the list.

Had having kids been on that list?

Probably not.

It wasn't something she'd let herself consider because to have a child, she needed a man. Although she could have chosen an unconventional route, but her mind hadn't gone there. Winter had had very few men in her life she could trust and more she couldn't. At least, she hadn't *believed* she could trust most men.

She'd grown up believing her mom didn't know who her father was and once she'd discovered the truth, she realized he was a man who wasn't worthy of the name. Not when it came to her sister. The men she'd dated hadn't helped her perception of the male gender. But now there was Harrison, who seemed to be trying to show her he could be there for her when it counted. Could she trust it would last?

With those thoughts swirling in her mind, she fell back to sleep.

A while later, Winter woke from a deep rest. A heavy blanket suffused her with a warmth she wasn't used to feeling. She forced her eyelids open and immediately realized the cause of the heat. Harrison's muscular body was wrapped around her, one arm over her side, his palm splayed on her belly beneath her tee-shirt which had ridden up above her panties. His bare chest pressed against her back and his cock nestled at her backside through the thickness of his sweats.

Within seconds, her body responded, awareness of him rushing through her veins. She took a deep breath, inhaled his masculine scent, and desire caused a sweet pulsing deep in her core, which scared her. She couldn't let herself feel this way about him again. Couldn't allow desire to ruin the understanding they'd come to about the baby and the friendly relationship she was coming to appreciate.

But she *did* desire him. Not in a happily ever after way. She wasn't sure she believed in such a thing. But in a turn around and crawl on top of him way. She wasn't a coward, and she'd been in this position with him before. Despite ending up pregnant, things between them had been easy and fun.

His hand dipped lower, his fingertips running along the edge of her bikini briefs and that's when she realized he was awake. She held her breath and he shifted his hand again. Her sex grew wet, and a low moan escaped the back of her throat.

He wrapped her tighter in his arms, his big palm settling on her belly. "My baby's really in there," he said in a gruff voice that hit all the right notes to turn her on even more.

She remained silent, aware this was *his* moment, his words a rhetorical statement she didn't need to respond to. But the protective way he touched her stomach, the awe in his voice? God, it was sexy. She needed to stop fighting herself. She wanted him and the hard ridge at her back told her he felt the same way. If there was a reason not to give in one more time, she couldn't think of one.

She rolled over and faced him. "At first, I didn't realize you were awake. Then your fingers and a certain body part let me know."

He let out a low chuckle, but it sounded strained, probably due to the erection he sported. "I'm very awake and aware of you." Those deep-blue eyes bored into hers. He paused as he studied her face as if attempting to read her mind, her intent and her desire.

He obviously saw what he needed because he joined their mouths together. His lips were soft but determined, a low-lying aggressive need evident behind the smooth motion of his mouth gliding over hers. His tongue slicked over her bottom lip, and she opened for him as she reciprocated the tangling of their tongues. An increasing need pulsed through her, and she slid her hands into his soft hair.

He groaned, and she expected him to push for more, to become more aggressive, but he took his time with long leisurely kisses, their mouths melding, her body a live wire of need. His hands glided down her sides until he clasped and held her hips in his palms, pulling her lower body into his.

His erection throbbed against her sex, but he

didn't force the issue, seemingly content for them to make out like teenagers. *This* hadn't been part of their past relationship. There'd been a rush toward satisfaction but even then, she was aware she felt more for him, and believed it was reciprocated.

But they'd both had their reasons for ignoring what was special between them and now she realized what she'd been missing with this languid, delicious meshing of mouths and bodies.

She began to move her hips, to gyrate and circle, seeking the pressure of his hard erection. He pulled her tighter against him and his rigid cock rubbed against her pussy, somehow finding her clit through the barrier of her panties and his sweatpants. He gave what she needed, and sensation shot through her, bringing her close to the edge.

Her hands tightened in his hair, and she pulled. "More."

"Yes." He slid a hand between them, dipping his fingers into her panties and she knew he found her wet with desire. "All for me, right, beautiful?" His deep voice worked as much magic as his body and fingers and then he pushed one inside her.

Her core clenched around him, but he pulled out and slid his now slick fingertip over her clit. She moaned and began to rock against him, seeking more of the waves he so easily created. He rubbed the tight bud with endless precision, bringing her higher and closer to exploding.

She slid her hands down and grasped his shoulders, digging her nails into his skin. Her eyes slid shut as she rocked her hips, rubbing her covered breasts against his chest while he worked her clit with one finger.

Her climax was close, and she shamelessly chased the feeling, hips rocking, her nipples abrading against her shirt.

"That's it, baby. Open those pretty eyes and come for me."

She forced her lids open and as a reward, he pressed his finger harder against her clit, then slid down to enter her again, triggering an orgasm that was out of this world.

"Yes, God, yes." She heard her own voice as waves crashed both around and through her. Stars lit up behind her eyes and she cried out her pleasure, letting the swell that kept coming take her higher.

Suddenly, he drove that long finger even deeper inside her. All the while, his gruff, arousing voice urged her on, somehow causing the orgasm to continue.

She panted and had just begun to come down to earth when he spoke. "Again," he said and curved his finger inside her, finding the perfect spot.

"Oh God."

"No, *me*," he said, his lips on her cheek as he rubbed inside her and triggered another climax on top of the last.

"Harrison," she groaned, burying her face in his warm neck and milking out every second she could before she collapsed against him.

He slid his finger out of her body, then pulled his hand from her panties. She felt the loss, but he held her so tight she didn't miss *him*.

His masculine scent surrounded her, and she wanted to keep her nose in his neck and smell him all day.

It took her a bit to come back to herself until finally she sighed and lifted her head from his shoulder, meeting his gaze. She felt her heated blush through her sweat-slicked skin.

"That was a surprise," he said.

She wrinkled her nose in confusion. "Me coming twice?" She asked the first thing going through her mind because a double orgasm had never been part of her repertoire.

He shook his head. "No, that's a testament to my talent," he said with a grin.

She wished she could deny that arrogant comment, but she'd just given him proof, so she merely rolled her eyes.

"I meant, I didn't expect us to end up in bed together and do anything other than sleep."

"I didn't either," she murmured.

"But here you are."

"And here *you* are," she said, reaching between them to slide her hand into his sweats and wrap her hand around his stiff cock. Turnaround was fair play and she *really* wanted to watch *his* face as he came.

He groaned and grasped her wrist, halting her movement. "This was about you, beautiful. I know how much the whole pregnancy, paparazzi, and accepting my help has you on edge. I don't want to rush you. I want you to take time, think, and see what we can be."

She blinked in surprise. *What guy didn't want to let a woman take care of him after he'd done the same for her?*

And what did he mean by, *let's see what we can be?*

Co-parents? Hookup buddies which, she had to admit, couldn't work for her on a permanent basis because if she let herself trust him completely, she could fall hard for the man, only to end up alone. Like her mother had been.

His cell trilled, interrupting her thoughts.

"I'm ignoring it." He reached over and tapped the side of the phone, sending the caller direct to voicemail and the cell went silent.

"Harrison, we need to agree that this was a one-time thing because I needed to stay here. And now I want to give back to you."

He frowned, but before he could reply, his phone rang again, and he cursed. "One sec," he said, an apology in his tone. He grabbed the phone and answered it. "What?" he snapped.

He sat upright in bed, obviously listening to the person on the other end.

"Got it. Yeah, come on over. Thanks, Zach." Harrison disconnected the call, placed the phone on the nightstand and turned to her.

"What's wrong?" She curled her legs beneath her.

Brows furrowed, he met her gaze. "I'd asked Zach to stop by your building and check things out. The reporters have thinned outside."

"I don't understand. That's good news, right?" What had him so concerned?

He nodded. "It is. It seems a politician was caught buying drugs from an undercover cop last night and most of the paparazzi have moved on, so you can go home," he said, and she was unable to read his feelings on the matter.

She told herself it was for the best. Staying with Harrison and sleeping in his bed would only lead to confusion and heartache later on.

"Zach also spoke to the doorman. He was going to ask the guy to call you when the coast was clear for you to get back to your life."

She tipped her head to the side. "I appreciate your family helping me." A warm, fuzzy feeling crowded her chest, one she wasn't used to feeling.

"You're one of us now, which is something you'll learn." He folded his arms across his chest. "The doorman gave him a envelope for you but with all the craziness of the reporters and the tenants complaining they couldn't get into the building—"

She winced, wondering how to make the inconvenience up to her neighbors.

"The doorman doesn't know or remember who left it. Zach is bringing it over now," Harrison said.

"I need to take a shower before he gets here." She flipped the covers off but before she could turn to climb out of the bed, Harrison had her lying flat and pinned beneath his big, hard body. "What are you doing?" she asked, breathless from the shock.

He gazed down at her, his expression serious. "Making sure we're on the same page before you leave my bed."

She swallowed hard but enjoyed every inch of him pressing her into the mattress. "What page is that?"

"I'm the last guy to look to the future and make promises. You know that. I know that. But we can agree the baby changed the playing field."

He paused, and she realized he was waiting for a reply, so she nodded. "It did," she agreed. "And that's how we ended up back here. Together. Let's not forget we agreed to short term, and things were over before I found out I was pregnant." She might as well tell him exactly where her head was when it came to them.

"I'm not going to deny the baby was the catalyst, but I never stopped thinking about you after we went our separate ways. Or after the engagement party."

When she'd gotten pregnant.

"You were always different than other women. You affected me in ways no one ever has before."

She blinked up at him, taking in his words. Was he saying they'd have reached out at some point, regardless?

"I just want you to keep that in mind." Leaning down, he brushed his lips over hers. "Go shower. I'll wait for Zach."

HARRISON WATCHED WINTER walk to the bathroom, his T-shirt falling to her mid-thigh, and he swallowed a groan, feeling possessive of the woman carrying his child. When his hand cupped her stomach, a wave of protectiveness washed over him and everything inside him stilled. In that silent moment, he let go of his past and his hectic childhood, all but forgot the woman who'd betrayed him, and he'd seen and felt his future.

He'd been a fool to let her walk away this summer when everything inside him screamed she was *the one*. But an inability to commit and worry about being hurt had held him back.

He didn't share Winter's fear of abandonment but understood it in a way most people couldn't. That was something he hadn't told her yet. She knew the facts about his mother, Audrey, but not the emotional wreckage she'd left behind. His past actually gave him hope that he could breach her walls.

The sound of the shower shook him out of his thoughts. Harrison wanted nothing more than to join Winter in the steamy room and watch the water rivulets run over her bare skin. Hell, he'd wanted to fuck her in his bed, but he'd thought before acting on impulse, and it was a damned good thing he had.

Because he was walking a tightrope with the mother-to-be of his baby. All her independence hid deep insecurities, and for now, he needed to focus on keeping her safe and in his life.

His cell buzzed, and a glance told him Zach was on his way up. Harrison climbed out of bed and pulled on a T-shirt he'd grabbed from his drawer. Then he strode to the foyer and met his brother at the door, opening it before Zach needed to knock.

Zach stepped inside. "Morning."

"Morning. How are you?" Harrison asked.

"I'm a little tired. How about some coffee for your errand running brother?" he asked as he shrugged off his leather jacket, hanging the garment in the closet by the front entrance.

Harrison turned and walked to the kitchen, his sibling behind him. "Come make yourself a cup."

As he entered, he saw Winter was already there. Her hair was damp, pulled into a low ponytail. She wore a pink top that ended at the waist, a thin strip of skin showing above the hem of the tight jeans encasing her sweet ass.

He swallowed a groan, not needing to give Zach any ammunition to give him shit.

Winter turned toward them and smiled. His cock immediately perked up, angry at him for not letting her reciprocate on him earlier.

"Hi, Zach. Can I make you some coffee?" she asked.

"Hey, sweetheart. Sure thing."

Harrison rolled his eyes at his brother's term of endearment. The man was a walking, talking Romeo.

"You can make your own," Harrison told him.

"That's okay. I've got it." She turned to prepare Zach a cup.

As she worked, his brother strode up beside her, propping a hip against the counter. "So, I take it you heard I went by your place?"

She nodded, waiting as the coffee dripped into the mug, pulled it out and put another cup in. "I appreciate it."

"Thanks." Zach winked at her, and Harrison shot his flirtatious brother a scowl.

She waited for the coffee to finish dripping and handed Harrison a cup of his own.

"Thanks, beautiful."

A pretty blush stained her cheeks. "I also heard you picked up something for me?" Zach handed her a large manila envelope with her name written on it in red crayon. "That's odd," she murmured.

Harrison agreed.

She peeled open the top and pulled out a letter with the same red crayon-colored writing on it. "I hope the baby looks like Harrison and *NOT* like you," she read, wrinkling her nose. "Well, that's rude." Sarcasm laced Winter's tone as she stared at the note Zach had given her.

Harrison tensed, hating how his life was negatively impacting her. She didn't need any more reasons to pull away.

She shrugged and tossed the paper on the counter, obviously not bothered, allowing him to relax, at least on that score.

"The wacko has a point," she said. "I hope the baby does have your Hollywood good looks."

"Winter thinks you're hot," Zach said with a grin. "Anyone have any popcorn? I'm here for the show."

"Don't let it go to your head," she said to Harrison, blushing at the same time Harrison scowled at his sibling.

"Asshole," he muttered.

Still, the thought that someone was sending Winter messages about the baby made his stomach churn. "Does this worry you at all?" he asked his brother, who'd made it his life's mission to help people in various ways.

Their family might come from hotel money and Asher had convinced them to invest in Dirty Dare Spirits, but each had their own talent that added to their finances. Jade and Nick worked at the hotels, Asher ran the spirits company, Harrison had made his name acting and now producing.

And Zach? He'd developed anti-hacking software a private company was willing to pay big bucks for, making him wealthy on his own. He'd bought the bar, and in his free time... Harrison wasn't sure *what* his brother did, but the man had skills.

Zach glanced at the note. "I wouldn't panic unless she keeps receiving them or the tenor escalates." He took a long sip of his coffee. "I would keep the bodyguard posted outside on her though."

"You have got to be kidding me! I can't just go back to my normal life without someone trailing along after me?" Winter asked, shock widening her eyes.

Shit. Harrison shot her an apologetic look, then ran a hand over his razor stubble. Though he wanted to argue with his brother, he couldn't. "Sorry. I have to agree with Zach."

"You're the woman who's having Hollywood's Hottest Playboy's baby," Zach said to her.

"Please tell me you're joking and they are not really saying that?"

"CGC is," Zach said.

She rolled her eyes. "Celebrity Gossip Central. Wonderful. And just as my notoriety for being the senator's illegitimate child was dying down." She wrapped her arms around herself, and he felt her pulling away.

"It's the price of fame. But anything I can do to help, let me know." Zach finished his coffee and placed the mug in the sink then ran water into it.

"Thank you," she said.

Zach winked. Again.

Harrison held back the need to throttle his sibling.

"It'll all sort itself out." Zach turned to face him. "Better to be me and stay under the radar."

"You call nearly getting yourself hauled in by the feds for hacking staying under the radar?" Harrison couldn't help but needle his sibling. It was how they showed their love.

"You did what?" Winter asked, her eyes wide.

Zach narrowed his gaze at Harrison for bringing up ancient history. While in college, his computer genius brother had hacked into a government site and gotten caught. Instead of arresting him, one of the agencies, Zach never revealed which one, had co-opted him into writing programs to keep people like himself out of restricted websites.

"I want to hear all about it." Winter was nearly bouncing on the balls of her feet. "That's an article in the making!"

Harrison could all but see the wheels turning in her head.

Zach met Winter's gaze and frowned. "The United States government does *not* want anyone knowing about hacks and leaks into their supposedly secure systems."

"Especially by a college kid," Harrison added, earning himself another glare from his brother. "Relax, Zach. She won't say anything."

"I promise," Winter said. "But can I get that story one day anyway?" Her interest had definitely been piqued, and it was a good tale.

Harrison strode over and hooked an arm around her waist. "Let it go for now," he whispered in her ear.

She sighed. "Okay, fine. So I can go home as long as I have a bodyguard with me?"

Not that he wanted her to leave, but he nodded. "That about sums it up."

"Okay, well, I won't be stupid and put us at risk." She rubbed her flat belly and Harrison's entire body hummed with unexpected pleasure at the sight.

She was so fucking gorgeous. Even makeup free, with her hair pulled up, he couldn't take his gaze off that perfect face set off by her big green eyes.

"I need to get to the bar," Zach said to Harrison. "And you know how to reach me. As for *you*..." He pointed to Winter. "Take care of my niece or nephew in there."

A smile lit her face, her hand still on her stomach. "I will."

Chapter Nine

TO WINTER'S RELIEF, after she left Harrison's apartment, her life quieted down. Morning sickness came and went, but it wasn't as bad as some women suffered, so she'd take it. Her bodyguard, a woman named Dana, had become her shadow and Winter enjoyed talking to her as they walked the city, or she took a ride share wherever she needed to go. In fact, Winter found Dana so fascinating she was now considering writing a piece on female security and bodyguards. Like most writers, Winter found fodder everywhere.

Harrison kept in touch constantly, be it by text, FaceTime or phone call. He didn't crowd her, but he had a way of letting her know he was thinking of her. And he'd invited her to the Hamptons to meet his family this coming weekend.

Agreeing hadn't been easy, but she'd done it. She already knew Zach was friendly and fun. Asher was uptight but completely on her side. She'd met Jade, and his stepmom, Serenity, at Nikki's engagement party. But Winter didn't know them well.

She certainly had no idea what his parents thought

of him having a baby with her or whether they liked her or not. Though she told herself it didn't matter... it did. She needed the rest of the Dare family to accept her, for no other reason than she'd be in their lives for a long time to come.

During the week, Winter met Nikki and Derek's fiancée, Jessica, for lunch. Jessica just happened to be on Winter's list of impressive women to interview. She'd launched a full-figured clothing and lingerie line, ran a boutique, and had just signed a deal to sell exclusive pieces of her lingerie to a high-end retailer, allowing curvaceous females to feel good about themselves and their bodies. She'd also weathered a scandal that might have taken a lesser woman down.

When Winter had expressed her nervousness over seeing Harrison's parents now that she was pregnant, Nikki had reassured her, explaining how amazing the family had acted when she'd met them for the first time.

Winter had come back with a throwaway comment that meeting families wasn't easy, which had Jessica squirming in her seat. Nikki then revealed how awful her mother had been when Derek had introduced her to Jessica. Their father had been pleasant, for which Winter was grateful. She supposed it was a plus in the man's favor.

Putting aside all other thoughts, Winter dressed for

lunch with a reporter friend she'd met when she worked at an online paper. She and her bodyguard walked to the restaurant, the cool fall air feeling good on her skin.

On the way, they passed a bookstore and Winter stopped in to buy a pregnancy book because the questions she had were growing. Like was it normal for her to have already lost her waistline and need new clothes? At what month would she see more than a blob on the screen or find out the sex of the baby? Did Harrison even want to know the gender? She did, so she could plan and buy exactly what she wanted.

Lunch was fun and relaxing and something she'd needed desperately. With Dana by her side, they walked back to Winter's building. She stopped by the mailroom before going upstairs and took out her mail. She had normal bills, junk mail, and *a manila envelope.* Her address was typed on a label with no return address in the upper left corner. She shivered a little and wondered what the crazy fans had to say to her this time? She shook her head. There were no letters written in crayon. Maybe it really was regular mail.

She slid the envelope into her large satchel, and they headed to her apartment. After thanking Dana, Winter unlocked her door and stepped inside, where she was greeted by an excited Panda, who barked and jumped up and down, wanting attention.

Winter picked up the pup and carried her to the kitchen. "Did you miss me?" she asked, waiting for the lick on her nose before putting her down. She glanced at her water bowl, seeing it was half full, then turned her attention to the mail.

"I'll talk to Dana about going out for a walk in a few minutes," she told the pup, talking to her as she usually did. "Let me just open this and see what I'm dealing with."

Picking a butter knife from the drawer, she sliced open the top of the envelope. "At least this came through regular mail, and nobody showed up at my apartment to hand deliver it."

She pulled out the contents and stared in shock at a sonogram. Not hers, this fetus was too far along, and she hadn't had an ultrasound yet. She could make out the shape of the baby's head and body. But the scary part, the more horrifying one, was the big X made of red tape over the photo.

A piece of paper had fallen onto the counter. She picked it up and unfolded it. Once again, the words were written in red crayon:

Some babies aren't meant to be born.

It would be better if you lost yours.

She let the paper drop to the counter and her stomach, which was always low-level queasy at best, threatened to revolt. This was a lot scarier and a more personal written attack than the last.

She strode to the door and flung it open. "Dana."

"What is it?" the woman asked, her hand instinctively going to her waist for her gun, immediately on guard.

"Come on in. Please."

The bodyguard, a pretty woman with pale-blonde hair and a confident demeanor, stepped into the apartment, then shut and locked the door behind her.

Once in the kitchen, Winter gestured to the envelope and its contents.

Dana took one look and scowled. "This is no joke."

"I didn't think it was." Winter wrapped her arms around herself and ignored the sonogram on the counter.

"It's a threat. You know I need to call it in, right?" Dana asked, already reaching for the phone in her pocket.

Winter nodded. "And I need to tell Harrison." He wouldn't take it well if he heard from Dana or her boss and not Winter herself.

Dana tipped her head, deferring to Winter. "Go ahead. I'll call from the living room." She stepped out, and Winter glanced down at her dog. "Don't sleep with a famous canine," she told Panda. "If they knock you up, you're only going to have more trouble."

Winter picked up her cell from the counter where she'd left it and pressed Harrison's name.

He answered immediately. "Hi. Everything okay?" he asked because *he* usually called her around bedtime.

"No." She gripped the phone tighter in her hand. "I received another note. This one came through the mail, and I think it's what television shows and profilers call escalating?" She heard the tremor in her voice and wished she'd been able to hide her emotions.

"I'll be there ASAP."

"You don't need to—"

"I said I am coming over." His tone brooked no argument, and she'd be lying if she said she wasn't relieved.

"Bring Dana inside with you," he said, his voice hard, his anger at whoever was tormenting her obvious.

"I already did."

"Good." He let out a long breath. "I'm sorry you're caught up in shit because of me," he muttered. "Now stay put and I'll see you soon." He ended the call, and she blew out a rough breath.

Once again, she looked at her dog. "Unless that famous canine is sexy and has a really gruff bark. Then you might reconsider," she told the Havanese.

Then Winter walked into her family room and sat down on the sofa to wait for Harrison to arrive.

HARRISON HAD BEEN with Zach when he got the call from Winter. Though he was grateful she'd thought to contact him immediately, he was pissed as hell his life was impacting hers at all.

No sooner had he hung up with her than the head of Alpha Security called, filling him in on the details of today's mailing. The sonogram and the note. *Some babies aren't meant to be born. It would be better if you lost yours.*

His stomach had lurched, and his hands curled into fists at his sides.

Zach left Raven in charge of the bar, and they headed for Winter's. He'd heard the panic in her voice when she'd called him, but she'd held it together. She'd even tried to convince him not to come over. As if he'd leave her to deal with a stalker on her own. *She was going to have to get used to him being there for her*, he thought, drumming his fingers on the side panel of the door.

"Calm down," Zach said as he drove his SUV uptown.

Harrison lifted an eyebrow. "A fan is threatening her, and we both know that shit can escalate. Winter is stuck with a bodyguard to walk her damn dog, or she has to hide out in her apartment. So you tell me. What's the upside to her being with me?"

"Is she *with you*? Or is she just having your baby?" Zach asked.

Harrison ground his teeth before answering. "Not the point."

"I think it is." After pulling to a stop at a red light, Zach turned to face him. "If she's just your baby mama, you can back off being there in person. You've already put security on her. Issue a joint statement about co-parenting and not being in a relationship which should de-escalate the crazies while we try and find the asshole. It'll definitely make your life easier if you don't have to watch over her twenty-four-seven."

"Fuck you, Zach," Harrison said, clenching his hands at his sides.

"Thought so." His brother let out a laugh. "I watched Nick and Asher fall for their women and you're just as obvious about Winter."

If Zach wasn't driving, Harrison might have decked him.

"I have a suggestion," Zach continued, oblivious

to the fact that he'd avoided being pummeled. "You're bringing her to the Hamptons this weekend, right?"

The light turned green, and Zach put his focus back on the road and the car sped forward.

"Yeah. She's coming with me."

Zach nodded. "After she talks to the cops, take her and go early."

Zach had called a friend on the force to meet them at Winter's apartment. Alpha Security and Zach had suggested, and Harrison agreed, that they needed to report the two incidents to the police and have the situation on record.

"Hole up in the Hamptons where it's safer. Take security but at least you'll see whomever it is coming instead of being in a city of millions."

Harrison nodded. "Makes sense."

Zach turned into the circular driveway of Winter's building and cut the engine. There wasn't a reporter in sight as a valet who would park the SUV approached.

Before they climbed out, Zach spoke once more. "And I figured out the upside to all this."

Harrison couldn't imagine what that could be. "You'll be alone in the Hamptons with the woman you're trying to win over. The reason sucks, but you can't deny the opportunity is golden."

That was Zach. Always looking at the bright side. It was an upside. For Harrison. For Winter, it remained to be seen.

They walked to the doorman. Although Harrison knew his name was now on her permanent list, he'd told her to instruct the doorman to have everyone call up and be approved before entering. Once given permission, they took the elevator upstairs. He was glad to see the security wasn't waiting in the hallway and was still inside the apartment.

At Winter's door, Harrison rang the bell and Dana's voice rang out. "Who is it?"

"Harrison."

The door opened, and Dana looked past the still-connected chain. Once she recognized him, she unlocked it and let them inside.

Zach immediately pulled Dana aside, but Harrison strode across the apartment, straight to Winter who had stood up from the sofa when he walked in.

She met his gaze and lifted her chin, conveying to him she could handle the situation but screw that. He reached her and pulled her into his arms. Her body remained stiff until he pressed his palm against her back. "I promise you'll be safe."

His words accomplished what his touch hadn't. She let out a tremulous sigh, her muscles relaxed, and she leaned into him, slowly wrapping her arms around his waist. "Thank you for coming."

"I wouldn't be anywhere else." Hearing footsteps,

he stepped back, keeping an arm around her, as he turned to face Zach and Dana.

"You okay, sweetheart?" Zach asked Winter.

She nodded. "Yes. It's just scary to think someone would take the time to send something like that."

"Unfortunately, that's the point. To scare you," Dana said.

"The police are on their way," Harrison said, holding onto her as she stiffened again.

She looked up at him. "It's notes and letters."

"And you're a smart reporter. You told me yourself. It's escalating. We need to get things on record in case... just to be safe."

"In case they try something in person."

"They won't get near you," Harrison promised. "We're taking every precaution, including making the authorities aware."

"I understand. And until they catch him or her? I need to be more careful? Not go out?"

Harrison shot his brother a pointed look. They were close enough that Zach took the hint.

"Dana, come show me the mail. We'll wait for the police in the kitchen," he said.

She nodded and followed him toward the smaller room on the other side of the apartment.

Once they left, Harrison touched Winter's shoulder. "Let's sit."

163

She curled her legs beneath her, and he studied her. She wore a lavender man-style shirt over what looked like a tank top and a pair of black leggings with a pair of vintage Doc Martens on her feet in pink and purple florals with black laces. Her hair was pulled into a low ponytail, soft tendrils falling around her pale face.

"Love the outfit," he said, hoping to put her at ease.

She smiled. "I have to wear my favorite clothes while I still can. My jeans don't close anymore." She treated him to an exaggerated pout, and he laughed.

For a brief second, even he'd forgotten why he was here, but the ringing of her phone reminded him. She glanced down and sighed. "Front desk," she said to Harrison. She answered the phone and instructed the doorman to let the police come up.

She disconnected and met Harrison's gaze.

"It's going to be okay."

She nodded. "I'm not scared. Am I freaked out? Yeah, I am. There are mentally ill people out there and I don't know what this one's end goal is. But I appreciate the protection." She tipped her head in the direction Dana had gone.

He had a minute, maybe less, to tell her his plan before they were joined by the cops. "After you give your statement, I'd like to pack up and go to my

Hamptons home tonight. Zach had a good point. You're safer where we know the people in town and have more control of who's coming and going. I have a fenced-in property and cameras."

She pursed her lips in thought.

He watched her, unable to read what she was thinking. He wanted to kiss those pretty pursed lips but now wasn't the time. If she agreed to leave the city, he'd have a few days before his family descended for the weekend to seduce her and cement his place in her life.

When she remained silent, he realized that instead of planning seduction and the future, he ought to be organizing his arguments in case she decided she didn't want to leave her home.

"You really think leaving makes the most sense?" she finally asked.

He nodded. "I do. More rooms to be in, you'll be able to take the dog on the property outside by yourself. I think, all around, it's a safer, more controllable environment." He already had Dana's boss headed to his place in the Hamptons to do a thorough check of his security system and cameras to make sure it was completely up to date and working as needed.

A knock sounded, followed by the ring of her doorbell.

She flinched at the noise, and he put a steadying

hand on her thigh. She might not be scared but she sure as fuck was jumpy.

"Well?" he asked before she decided to go to greet her company.

"Okay," she said as she rose to her feet. "We can go to your Hamptons house."

Relief flooded him for reasons that went far beyond her safety, even if that always came first. "Good. Let's get the interview with the police over with. Then you can pack."

TALKING TO THE police hadn't been an experience Winter wanted to repeat. There had been two detectives, one a friend of Zach's and the other, his more uptight partner. While Remy Sterling had been interested in every last detail Winter and Harrison had to offer, Detective Sterling's partner thought they were wasting their time on *fan mail*.

They'd asked if she had any enemies. It was all she could do not to laugh. Other than the occasional tough question to someone she was interviewing, Winter wasn't confrontational. Well, unless she counted the time she'd walked into Senator Bettencourt's home and informed him and his wife she was the daughter Collette had wanted Winter's mother to abort. But she'd chosen not to mention that to the police. Her personal life wasn't up for Detective Asshole's dissection.

More than once, she'd had to grab Harrison's hand and squeeze tight to prevent him from allowing a verbal confrontation to escalate thanks to his frustration with the disinterested detective. Fed up himself, Zach had cleared his throat and his friend had then *strongly suggested* his partner take a walk and let him finish getting details.

Detective Sterling, who, after his partner had stormed off, had insisted Winter call him Remy, had apologized and assured her that he would take the case seriously. Apparently Detective Asshole—the nickname bestowed upon him by Harrison—had a bias against actors since his wife had cheated on him with a Broadway performer.

Both Remy and Zach swore they'd handle things, and she believed them. Harrison had quietly assured her that given the men's close friendship, they would be working together off the books.

Zach left not long after Remy and Dana had also ended her shift and said goodbye. Harrison's security detail was waiting outside, and they didn't need two people when she and Harrison would be together.

Packing up for an extended time away wasn't simple. Winter needed everything for both herself and

Panda, along with her laptop and headphones for work, and her eReader for the downtime she assumed she would have. After she'd gathered their things, Harrison had a driver and car waiting to take them to his apartment so he could do the same. Although he packed up much less since he had clothing and necessities at his house.

While he took care of packing at his apartment, Winter called Nikki, then Derek, to let them know the plan. To her shock, Nikki had received a call from her mother, warning her to stay away from the *home-wrecking child of her father's mistress*. Nikki had asked her mother not to call her again. She wasn't ready to deal with her, reminding Winter of how much she'd lucked out in the mom department. She might not have grown up with a father, but she'd had a loving, caring parent. Who she missed badly.

Winter supposed that was why she texted the senator about her intention to leave town. She really couldn't say why else she'd bother but she hoped maybe he'd want to know where she was going. She left out the whys of it all. They weren't close enough for her to bring him into the chaos.

Then she touched base with her friend and mentor. Erin was beside herself to hear what Winter was going through. She'd spoken to Erin after the pregnancy news had broken in the media, but Erin hadn't been aware of her stalker issue. Winter felt more comfortable letting Erin know than the senator. Her father. Gah. She needed to decide what he was to her and how to think of him.

There were so many things swirling through her brain she barely had time to process the fact that she and Harrison were going back to the scene of the crime. So to speak. His luxurious home where he'd had the engagement party for Nikki and Asher, and where she'd fallen into bed with him again. And wound up pregnant.

Her stomach flipped at the notion of them alone and the possibilities of what could happen between them. He had a hot tub, which she knew from reading online articles wasn't healthy to use during pregnancy, a pool which it was too cold outside to enjoy, and a massive media room. His home theater, with a full wall-to-wall LED screen, had a large couch with reclining seats and was an extremely comfortable space for sex. This, she knew firsthand.

Nerves and nausea were her companions as the driver loaded his things beside hers in the trunk. Then she and Harrison, along with Panda, climbed into the back seat for the drive. She'd ended up putting her head in his lap and stretched out to sleep while the dog settled between her legs.

And Harrison's fingers curled in her hair.

She felt safe, cared for and more peaceful than she'd expected given the day's events. He'd shown up when she needed him. Been there for her even though one of the detectives thought they were exaggerating the threat. And he was taking her away to a place he believed she would be safe.

Her hand came to rest on her stomach as her eyes slowly closed, exhaustion overtaking her.

HARRISON SIFTED HIS fingers through Winter's hair as she slept. A warmth unlike anything he'd felt before settled in his chest. Even if she weren't carrying his baby, he would protect her and want her the same way. Which meant he was damned lucky he had potent sperm or whatever had happened to push them together. Or else he might never have gotten his shit together and made the move.

He glanced at her hand splayed across her belly and his heart, that thing he'd never given a thought to before, squeezed harder. She was his. And so was the baby growing inside her. They were the family he hadn't been aware of wanting. Now they were what he needed.

He intended to make damned sure they stayed safe.

By the time they arrived at his East Hamptons home, night had fallen. The driver shut off the engine and walked around to open his door.

"Can you take her, please?" Harrison handed Panda's leash to Bruce, a great guy who drove for whatever family member needed him. "If you put her down on the ground, she'll probably go."

"No problem."

Bruce took the dog for a walk and Harrison stroked a hand over Winter's cheek. "Wake up, beautiful."

Her dark lashes fluttered, and those gorgeous green eyes settled on his face.

"We're here," he said.

She pushed herself to a sitting position, and he helped her out of the car. Morgan, the bodyguard who'd started the night shift an hour early, had followed behind them in his own car and pulled in alongside the parked car just as Bruce returned with Panda.

"She did her business," he said, giving Winter the leash.

"Thank you," she said.

"My pleasure, ma'am." He smiled and strode to the open trunk to unload the bags and suitcases.

Harrison took Winter's hand and led her to the door. Morgan had already jogged ahead and stood beside them as Harrison unlocked the door and unset the alarm.

Obviously certain the house was secure, Morgan stepped aside for Harrison and Winter to enter. A little while later, all the bags were in the correct rooms, divided between his and the kitchen for Panda's food and bowls. They hadn't discussed sleeping arrangements, and this house had four guestrooms.

Rooms he hoped she wouldn't want to use.

Bruce left, taking the car back to the city. Harrison kept a convertible here to use when he was in town. Already he was mentally planning on what SUV he'd need to buy for both here and Manhattan since a family of three needed room for a car seat.

Jesus. He ignored the occasional flash of nerves that came when he thought about the baby and specific things that would change. Told himself it was normal. And knew he had a conversation or twelve with his father and his engaged or married brothers in his future. They'd know how to keep him calm.

A look outside told him that Morgan had taken up his spot outside, an app with a full view of all the property cameras on his cell phone.

He walked into the kitchen to find Winter staring into the refrigerator.

"It's fully stocked." Surprise echoed in her voice.

"While I was packing, I called the caretakers and

told them I was coming."

She turned to him, eyes wide. "And they provided everything you needed that quickly?"

He shrugged, knowing better than to throw out a remark that would make him sound exactly like what he was. Spoiled. "I'm fortunate to employ good people." And he paid them well for last-minute trips like this one. "I'm pretty sure there's a homemade lasagna in there for tonight if you're hungry."

Before she could answer, her stomach replied for her with a loud growl. She pressed against her belly and her cheeks flushed red.

"I'll take that to mean you're both starving." He winked and stepped around her to find the food in the fridge. "Mrs. Baker is my housekeeper. She owns a cleaning company and sends a crew in once a week."

"It makes sense that you'd have someone who checks in on things," Winter said.

While he spoke, he found their dinner and placed it on the counter, then turned on the oven to preheat it. "When I let her know I'm coming, she stocks the food and whatever else I need. She also insists on making me an easy-to-heat-up dinner. No matter how much short notice I give her."

"That's nice of her," Winter mused.

He nodded. "She's a good businesswoman. She's licensed and insured for all she does. But the little details like cooking? That's Mrs. Baker's pure love of people. Her husband is wheelchair bound, and she takes care of him, too. She says she only cooks extra for clients she likes."

Winter laughed. "And how many of those people are there? Wait. Let me guess. They're all named Dare."

He grinned. "And Kingston. As you know from the interview, Xander and Sasha Kingston have a place here, so do Dash and Cassidy Kingston, as well as her brother, Axel Forrester, The Original Kings' drummer. He bought a house after he married the local vet, Dr. Tara Stillman. Asher purchased something after he and Nikki got together. Renovations are almost done on their place."

Harrison glanced down at Panda who'd settled on the cool tile floor. "You're in good hands if you need them. Tara is just a phone call away." He spoke to the pup but was really reassuring Winter. "But back to Mrs. Baker's cooking, there's also me. That's five clients that I know of."

Winter rolled her eyes, but he sensed she liked his story.

"I hope I get to meet her while I'm here," she said.

"I'm sure that can be arranged."

She braced her hands on her hips and looked around. "So where are the dishes? I'll set the table while we're waiting for the oven to heat."

He opened his mouth to insist he could handle it, then tell her to sit down, but she shook her head at him. "I slept the entire ride here. I can help." Her tone and narrowed eyes dared him to disagree.

Knowing better than to argue, he pointed to the cabinet above the dishwasher. "Dishes there. And the silverware is in this drawer." He pulled it open to show her.

They worked like a well-oiled team and once he put the food in the oven, they sat beside each other on barstools by the center island.

"So, I noticed you put my bags in your room." Winter didn't beat around the bush.

He liked that she confronted things head-on. He might as well handle her the same way. "Because that's where I want you to stay."

She leaned an elbow on the gray granite countertop with white swirls in the pattern and propped her chin on her hand. "What are you saying?" she asked in a suddenly husky voice.

He took up the same position and leaned in close. "I'm saying I want you. And judging by your reaction to me the other morning in my bed, I think you want the same thing."

Chapter Ten

WINTER COULDN'T FIND it in her heart to deny Harrison's claim. She did want him. Which was how she found her things unpacked in his room and herself in his bed. Although she'd brought her own clothing, he'd offered her one of his T-shirts to sleep in, and she'd gladly accepted. Even the scent of his laundry detergent made her feel like she was enveloped by him, and she felt both protected and aroused.

He'd taken Panda for her last walk, letting her out in the backyard while she got ready for bed. Though Panda was used to sleeping beside her, she was also content in her dog bed. Once they'd returned, Harrison went into the bathroom and the dog happily settled into the bed Harrison had placed across the room and passed out.

She waited, nerves wreaking havoc with her stomach, but she'd made her choice. While she was in the Hamptons, she would be in Harrison's bed. *Where had she heard that before*, she thought wryly, just as the bathroom door opened and the man on her mind walked out.

He wore a pair of boxer briefs and nothing more,

his muscular body sexy and well-toned. Everything about him appealed to her and desire was like a flash fire in her veins. And from the heated look in his gaze as he approached, he wasn't coming to bed to sleep.

He paused at the edge of the mattress and met her gaze. "We're on the same page?"

She nodded. "We are." As she spoke, her lower body softened, and arousal coated her panties. "What are you waiting for?" she asked, her voice sounding surprisingly husky.

His eyes darkened with need, and he crooked a finger her way. She'd already decided she was all in, so she pushed the covers off her legs and slid toward where he waited. Obviously impatient, he grasped her ankles and pulled her closer.

Hooking his fingers in her barely there panties, he slid them over her legs and dropped the pair onto the floor, exposing her to his hungry stare.

She had no time to be embarrassed before he dropped to his knees, placed her legs over his shoulders and dove in like a starving man. He licked her sex, remembering exactly what she both needed and liked.

He sucked her outer lips, pulling one, then the other into his mouth then nipped at each. She moaned and when she arched her back, he grasped her hips, angling her so he could spear his tongue inside, causing her to lose control. She rocked her lower body, rubbing her sex against his mouth, seeking more friction.

He gave her what she needed. His tongue traveled a path from her core to her clit and fluttered against the perfect spot, causing her to see stars.

"More," she begged him, and he complied, sliding one finger inside her, curving it and rubbing her G-spot. His talented tongue flickered over her clit, urging her on.

She went *soaring*. Her climax rocked her completely and she rode the waves until she thought she might pass out. When she came to, he'd lowered her legs and had opened the nightstand drawer. He held a condom in his hand.

"I'm already pregnant," she said, the words spilling out.

His eyes flared with desire, and she couldn't deny the sudden need to feel him bare inside her and her pussy clenched at the thought.

"I've never gone without one," he said in a gruff voice. "Never wanted to... until you."

His words impacted her deeply.

He ran his hand over her calf, his gaze never leaving hers. "I know I'm clean."

On that, she trusted him completely. "I am too," she murmured.

She hadn't been with anyone long before getting

involved with Harrison and she'd had her yearly physical prior to ever meeting him.

"So I don't need it?" He still held the condom in his hand.

"No, you don't," she said, knowing this one act might bring her closer to the man she was trying to keep behind an emotional wall.

HARRISON TOSSED THE protection back into the drawer, taking a second to calm himself down. While he wanted to feel Winter's warm, wet walls clench around him, he refused to take her like a rutting asshole. She was pregnant with his baby. More precious to him than a quick fuck. Not that she'd want to hear his sappy thoughts when he still saw the emotional struggle behind her emerald eyes.

Her taste lingered on his lips, and the sound of her moans and sighs as she came still rang in his ears. But he wanted to savor tonight as if it were their first time. As far as he was concerned, given their changing dynamic, it might as well be.

"Harrison?"

Her voice brought him out of his thoughts, and he glanced her way. Her dark hair was a sultry tangle around her flushed face. Her lips were damp and slightly parted. And the T-shirt had ridden above her waist, revealing her sex, glistening from the combination of his mouth and her juices. The sight made him aware of the ache in his dick.

"Scoot back," he said in a rough voice.

She did as he commanded until she was against the pillows, watching him intently.

"Now take off your shirt." He stripped naked while she did the same, her breasts bouncing as she tossed the garment onto the floor.

As he joined her on the bed, she reached out and wrapped her hand around his straining cock.

He closed his eyes and let himself enjoy a few moments of pleasure before he opened them again and grasped her wrist. "Unless you want this over with now, you need to stop."

She glanced down and her gaze widened at the sight of pre-come on the head of his dick. Without warning, she sat up, leaned forward, and licked it off, moaning as she sat up again, a Cheshire Cat grin on her pretty face.

His entire body vibrated with need, and he nudged her shoulders. Taking his cue, she lay back on the bed. He glanced at her body, realizing for the first time, her breasts were fuller and her waist was less defined. She was still fucking gorgeous.

Leaning over, he licked one nipple, pulling the

tight bud into his mouth and scraping with his teeth.

She gripped his shoulders, her long nails digging in deep. "Oh my God. I'm so sensitive," she moaned.

He lightened his touch and gently sucked and licked, shocked when her hips began to rotate beneath him. Her wet heat rubbed against his cock, and he couldn't wait any longer. He raised his hips and settled himself at her entrance.

Their eyes met, and he entered her, inch by inch. Sweat beaded on his forehead and over his body. Holding back was torture.

"What's with the slow motion?" she asked. "The Harrison I remember had power moves." She arched a sexy eyebrow at him and waited for an answer.

Which he didn't have. He couldn't come up with a way to explain that he was being delicate with her. It was as new a situation to him as it was to her.

"I'm pregnant, not breakable," she said, figuring out the problem on her own. "And I refuse to be treated like I am."

Before he could react, she slid out from beneath him. "Flip onto your back, Harrison." She nudged his shoulder, not that he needed convincing, and he sprawled on his back.

She straddled him, her hands on his shoulders. Leaning over him, she brought her lips close to his. "Are we clear?" she asked in a sexy voice.

"Crystal," he said. God, she turned him on.

"Good." She treated him to a cheeky grin as she grasped his cock in one hand, placed him at her entrance, and dropped down, swallowing him inside her completely.

Holy shit. He closed his eyes and tried to process the feeling of her slick walls clasping his bare cock in her wet heat.

"Now, I can be on top…" Her voice trailed off, and she pushed up on her knees, lifting herself until he almost slipped out of her heavenly body, then she slid back down again, and he groaned. "Or you can get over your ridiculous concerns and *you* can fu—"

He thrust his hips upward, completely willing to let her ride him. Her eyes gleamed, and she began to move, dragging herself up and dropping back down, picking up a rhythm that had his eyes rolling back in his head. He grasped her hips and held on, shifting his lower body in time to her movements, all but slamming into her despite his self-imposed promise to be gentle.

Her core squeezed his cock tight, and he nearly came from the pleasure, but he held out, determined to let her climax first. He slid his hands up her sides and brushed his fingertips beneath her breasts before rubbing his thumbs over her sensitive nipples, giving each the attention they deserved.

"That's so good." Her tone was thick with desire.

He pressed his thumbs into the tight buds, and her pussy squeezed him tight. "And you feel so fucking good."

"So do you," she said, rocking her hips and rubbing her clit against his pubic bone with each shift forward.

He tightened his abs and pushed himself to a sitting position, grinding their lower bodies together. Her eyes glazed over, and she wrapped her arms around his neck, holding him close, her breasts rubbing against his hair-roughened chest.

"Yes," she said, her body trembling, her orgasm obviously close.

He knew what would tip her over the edge. He eased back, separating them so he could dip his head and pull one tight nipple into his mouth. He sucked hard, tweaking the other with his finger and twisting hard.

"Oh my God, Harrison." She drew out his name and stilled for a brief second before she rocked herself into him over and over, riding out her climax while he forced himself to hold back.

They weren't finished yet. Their bodies still connected, he flipped her onto her back and began to pound into her hard and deep. Clasping their fingers together, he drew her arms above her head and ground their bodies together, his climax hitting him like a freight train. And when he came, his hot come spurt inside her, claiming her, even if she wasn't aware of it yet.

After they'd cleaned up, she didn't fight him when he pulled her into his arms. She fell asleep fast, leaving him to breathe in her intoxicating coconut scent mixed with the lingering smell of sex in the air around them. He fell asleep to the thought that he could get used to her in his bed and in his life.

The next morning, he woke up early and slipped out from beneath the covers, leaving Winter to sleep. He let the dog out back and returned for a quick shower.

He pulled on a pair of track pants and strode into the kitchen, realizing too late he smelled coffee before he walked into the room.

His gaze came to rest on Zach. "Oh hell no. How did you even get inside? I changed the lock the last time you let yourself in."

Zach liked to practice his skills on his siblings' homes. It was annoying as fuck. "Did you really think an electronic keypad would stop me?"

"I had high hopes. What would you suggest I try next?" Harrison asked, tempted to slap the smirk off his brother's face.

His brother lifted one shoulder and took a sip of

coffee from one of Harrison's mugs. "If you want to make it challenging, try a fingerprint."

Harrison groaned. "It wasn't a serious question. Where was the bodyguard?" He assumed Morgan had switched places with someone for the day shift.

"Watching me," Zach said with a shrug.

Whenever the family used the security company, they had the names of everyone allowed in without calling first. And Zach, of course, was friendly with them all.

"I'm kidding, by the way. Today I used my key."

Harrison rubbed his eyes, a headache already forming. He walked to the dog food and Panda ran up to him, jumping on her hind legs. "Thanks for letting her inside," he muttered.

"No problem."

He put the dog's food into the bowl and set it on the floor. Then he made himself a cup of coffee. "You aren't supposed to be here until the weekend. When Mom and Dad come," he said to Zach. "What gives?"

He'd planned on having two days alone with Winter before his family showed up en masse. Unfortunately, he was the only one of the Dares with a Hamptons house anyone could stay in. Asher's was still under construction and though he and Nikki could stay in one part, he couldn't yet have company. Everyone had planned on staying with him. Something he hadn't explained to Winter yet because he knew she'd be overwhelmed.

"I'm here because I wanted you two to have back-up." Zach shrugged. "Just in case."

Before Harrison could either thank Zach for caring or call him out on his bullshit because they trusted Alpha Security, Panda ran toward the kitchen entry-way.

"Zach!" Winter stepped into the room wearing Harrison's T-shirt and nothing more. His *white* T-shirt which showed her pert nipples through the soft, thin material. "I didn't know you were coming today!" She immediately bent down and picked up Panda, holding her against her chest and letting Harrison breathe more easily.

He shot his sibling a glare.

Zach grinned. "Morning, pretty girl. Sorry. Didn't mean to disturb you." He stepped down from the stool. "I'll go hang out with Chris. He's taking the day shift. Morgan has some time off, then he'll be back for his usual times."

At least his brother had the decency to leave them alone.

The doorbell rang, and suddenly he heard familiar voices talking. Too many voices. "Why did I give everyone a damned key?" Harrison muttered.

Because his house was used by all of his family

members if they decided to spend time here when Harrison was in the city. Or join him during the summer. It was just how they rolled... and that ended now.

Winter's eyes opened wide at the sound of voices, and she let out a squeak. "I need to get dressed!" Keeping Panda tucked against her chest, she spun and rushed past him, heading out the back entrance to the room that avoided the front door.

Zach met his gaze and shrugged. "Sorry, man. The parents will explain."

Harrison groaned and walked out to deal with his family.

★ ★ ★

WINTER RUSHED BACK to the bedroom and shut the door, locking it behind her. His family was... a lot. And she hadn't even spent time with them yet.

She placed Panda on the floor and drew a deep breath, deciding to prioritize her thoughts before the buzzing in her head drove her insane. First, she needed to shower before she faced the Dares. When she'd woken up alone, she'd had time to remember being with Harrison. Feeling him deep inside her had been beyond orgasmic. Actually, it had been multi-orgasmic, and that included when he'd woken her up in the middle of the night by sliding inside her.

He'd tried to be gentle, and she couldn't deny that his worrying about her and the baby's well-being touched her heart. The same heart she was trying to hold on to and not hand over to the man on a silver platter. But she'd also decided not to overthink and just enjoy. It had worked well for her last night, so she'd decided to join him in the kitchen and see if he was in the mood for some morning sex. Instead, she'd seen his brother. And then she'd heard their family.

She took a long, hot shower, washed her hair, then took the time to blow dry it and put on some makeup before going back out to meet Harrison's family. For the first time that morning, she picked up her phone and saw Nikki had texted her with a heads-up that the family was coming to the Hamptons. Asher had a business meeting, and she promised they'd be there later that day. And she'd be staying in a hotel.

Where was the rest of the family going to sleep? She drew a deep breath and walked into the kitchen where Serenity and Jade were making breakfast.

Serenity turned and a smile lit her face. "Winter! Come on in. I'm making eggs and bacon and pancakes. Because everyone likes something different."

"Hi, Winter." Jade waved from where she stood by the extra-large, overly stocked refrigerator. Winter probably should have realized the sheer amount of food meant company was coming but Harrison had said it wasn't until the weekend.

Jade's baby bump was big, giving Winter a glimpse of how her body would change.

"Morning." Winter stepped into the kitchen and Panda ran for her water bowl. "I didn't realize you were all coming today."

Serenity piled more pancakes on a large plate. "It was a last-minute decision, to be honest. We have a surprise to tell everyone and... well, you'll see soon."

"Where are the guys?" Winter asked.

"In the family room talking," Jade said. She shut the fridge door with her foot and carried an orange juice container to the already set table.

"Can I help?" she asked, wanting to feel useful.

Jade shook her head. "Serenity likes to do it all," she said, love in her voice. "I've learned to let her."

"I figured you're all busy during the week with work, so if we're going to show up and impose, I might as well be useful. The kids always love family breakfast, so... why not?"

Jade grinned and patted Winter on the shoulder. "You'll get used to it," she promised.

"Oh, I... I'm only here because I'm having a—"

"Stalker issue." Zach appeared seemingly out of nowhere, strode over to the plate warmer and snagged a piece of bacon to crunch on.

Serenity smacked his hand and laughed. "Wait for everyone else and use the tongs, you savage."

"He's always been the animal of the family." Jade snickered behind his back.

"It's not a stalker issue, per se—"

"We don't know what it is, so we're being careful, yes?" Zach asked, as if confirming she understood the potential severity of her situation.

She nodded. "Yes, of course. I'm just…" Feeling like an intruder in the family despite having been here before them.

"We're a lot," Jade said, her hand on her belly.

"Nikki tells me you're seven months along," she said to Jade.

The pretty woman with her blonde hair pulled back in a ponytail smiled. "Yes, so you can ask me anything, and I'll likely already have the answer."

Winter's cheeks flushed with heat. "I appreciate that. I've been reading books."

Jade laughed. "Trust me when I tell you, there are things you may want to know you won't get in a book. I'll give you my number. Call or text me any time." She poured a glass of orange juice which Zach immediately picked up and drained most of in three large gulps.

"Hey! That was for me and the baby!" Jade exclaimed.

"And I don't have cooties." He winked at his sister.

Jade's *ew* expression was priceless. "I'm not drinking your backwash, Zach."

They continued to bicker until Serenity stepped between them. "What are you, ten? Behave in front of company." She smiled warmly at Winter, who was taking in the whole, big family dynamic.

She knew she was staring, but it was a combination of things that had her breath coming in shallow pants. She'd never experienced having siblings growing up. Having someone besides her adult parent to talk to and joke with. And she'd never realized what she'd been missing. Until now.

Then there was the sudden pang of loss she experienced while watching them. God, she missed her mother. If Juliana were here, Winter wouldn't feel so alone with the pregnancy. Harrison had stepped up for her, and Nikki and Derek too, but her mother had been… her mother. Irreplaceable.

In so many ways, Winter was still getting to know her own siblings. They'd never shared… *this.*

Just then, the men walked in, talking to each other and laughing, the fun, teasing tones and closeness equally as evident.

And suddenly the shortness of breath became a minor panic attack that threatened to turn Winter into a crying mess. Out of nowhere. *This had to be what the books meant by pregnancy hormones*, she thought, horrified at the notion of breaking down in front of strangers.

"Winter?" Harrison had walked over to her, and she hadn't noticed.

She forced a smile.

"Are you okay?" His concerned expression, eyebrows drawn together and the worried frown on his face, nearly did her in.

Unable to speak, she nodded. "I just need a minute," she whispered, and to her humiliation and shock, she fled the room.

HARRISON STARED AFTER Winter then turned to his unexpected visitors, reminding himself he loved his family dearly. "What just happened?"

They looked at him in silence until Jade spoke up. "Nothing, honestly. Zach and I were… bickering about food. Mom was cooking and telling us to behave. I think we overwhelmed Winter," Jade said, her expression worried.

Zach glanced at him. "I didn't think anything of it. I walked in just as Winter asked if she could help in the kitchen."

"I said Mom likes to do it all, and she'd get used to it," Jade picked up the story as her husband, Knox, slipped an arm around her waist.

The words *getting used to it* had probably panicked Winter, who didn't believe she'd be part of his family as anything other than his baby's mother. *Shit*, he thought.

"Then Winter said something about only being here because..." Jade's words trailed off.

"I didn't let her finish," Zach said. "I jumped in and explained she had a stalker issue." He shrugged. "Again, I didn't mean anything by it."

Harrison groaned. And he'd been right. She'd been overwhelmed, yes, but had also felt alone.

"I think she panicked for some reason," Jade said. "She was breathing heavily and let's face it, I recognize the signs."

Harrison nodded and groaned. His sister had grown up with stress and panic attacks after their mother had abandoned them along with other, more complicated, reasons. And she'd nailed Winter's reaction.

"Winter grew up an only child. A very independent only child," he explained, planning to only give his family the bare basics and not overstep Winter's boundaries. "But Jade has a point. As a whole, we're a lot." He looked at his father, Michael and raised his eyebrows. "And I still don't know why you're here today and didn't wait for the weekend?"

Harrison had asked already. His father had insisted he would explain later.

"Let's wait for Asher and Nikki," Michael said again. "I want to tell you all together. The boys are away at college and Layla stayed at a friend's so she didn't miss school. We'll give them the news when we get home."

Resigned, Harrison glanced at Serenity. "Is breakfast ready?"

She nodded.

"Okay. Let me go get Winter and we can eat." He needed to make sure she understood some things about them and his big, crazy family.

★　★　★

As soon as Winter calmed down, she regretted running from the kitchen and leaving herself open to discussion behind her back. She wasn't typically a coward, but she'd never had a true panic attack before, either. She'd put a glass of water by her bedside and took a long sip, then walked to the window that overlooked a lush yard with a pool. One that would get covered for the snowy season soon.

She heard Harrison's footsteps and then felt his heat against her back.

His strong palms came to rest on her shoulders.

"They're overwhelming." He obviously spoke about his family.

"They're amazing. There are just a lot of them," she murmured. "And this isn't everyone. Plus, my mom was a working mom. She didn't make us breakfast. She took us to a diner for a special splurge."

"Serenity started out as the nanny," he said. "Besides, every parent is different. Not better or worse."

She swallowed hard. The lump in her throat had returned. "I miss her."

He shifted his hands and rubbed his thumbs against her neck. "I know. When my mom walked out, I kept waiting for her to come back. I prayed every night and kept asking my brothers when. When was Mom coming home? Why did she leave? Even if they knew, what could they tell a six-year-old?"

She tipped her head back and rested against his chest. "That's awful."

"Yeah, well, after she… died, I was having a hard time at school because I was into theater and the other guys made fun of me. I was depressed, and I admitted to Asher I was scared I'd do what my mother did."

She sucked in a startled breath.

"It was just a kid thing. I didn't ever contemplate suicide, I was just freaked out by what Mom… what happened. Asher didn't know that Jade was sitting in a huge chair, reading. We couldn't see her. And he said

196

it only happened to girls. He was a kid, too. He just wanted to calm me down."

She closed her eyes. "Oh, no."

From behind her, she felt his nod. "Jade had her first migraine headache that night. I think the panic attacks started later. My point is, there are a lot of us, but we are an understanding bunch."

Her heart broke for a young Jade who'd lost her mother and believed such wrong information for what had probably been way too long. "I like your family. They're good people and they've been so kind. But I'm not one of them and when Jade said I'd get used to it... meaning them... I—"

He spun her around, cutting her off mid-sentence. "You damn well are one of us," he said and sealed his mouth over hers.

He kissed her, a deep, thorough kiss obviously meant to express more than she was ready to deal with, but she couldn't deny him. Lifting onto her toes, she met his tongue with hers. Their bodies aligned, his need obvious thanks to the hard erection pressing insistently against her belly. Warmth spread like liquid through her veins, and she could no longer think or worry at all.

He wrapped an arm around her back and pulled her closer when a knock sounded on the bedroom door.

She turned her head toward the *open* bedroom door.

"Breakfast is getting cold." Zach stood in the entryway, his hand raised and an unapologetic grin on his face.

"Cockblocker," Harrison muttered, still holding her around the waist.

Winter felt her cheeks burn and glared at his brother. Zach merely winked at her.

"I cannot wait until it's your turn to find a woman who matters, and I can give you this much shit," Harrison muttered.

She mattered. The word pinged in her brain.

Zack fake choked. "There hasn't been anyone who interested me that way since…" He shook his head. "Never mind. I'll see you in the kitchen," he muttered and walked out.

"What was that all about?" she asked.

"That's a story too long for now." Harrison grasped her hand, looking at her through his sexy indigo gaze.

And when her tongue slid over her lips, those eyes darkened with desire. *Which was good*, she thought, because the same yearning was still pulsing through her body, along with confusion about what was going on between them.

"Are you up to going back in to eat?" he asked.

Still dazed, she managed to nod.

Chapter Eleven

HOURS LATER AND Winter's head still spun from Harrison's words and that kiss. Thank goodness Nikki and Asher showed up a few hours after breakfast, which gave Winter the emotional support she needed. An hour after that, a pregnant Aurora, Harrison's brother and Jade's twin, Nick, and their daughter, Leah, arrived. At Michael and Serenity's request, they all gathered in the family room.

Leah, an adorable six-year-old, bounced into the house, wearing a pair of leopard print leggings, a long black T-shirt and a pink and black fleece jacket with a pair of shimmery pink Doc Martens on her feet.

She paraded around the room, collecting hugs and kisses from her grandparents and all her aunts and uncles, finally reaching Harrison and Winter.

"Hi, Leah," Winter said.

"Who are you?" she asked, wrinkling her nose up at Winter, a curious expression on her face.

"Leah, ask that question nicely," Aurora said, shooting Winter an apologetic glance.

Winter waved a hand through the air, indicating it was fine. "I'm Winter."

"Like the season? We learned them in school."

Winter grinned. "Just like the season."

"Well, it's fall now," Leah informed her. "I like your name."

Harrison grasped Winter's hand. "Winter is my girlfriend," he told Leah.

This was news to Winter, but she didn't want to question him in front of his family, who appeared equally stunned, given their wide-eyed stares.

Winter wanted to take the focus off the subject. "You know, Leah, I have a flowered pair of Doc Martens, but I love yours."

"Ooh! Mommy, I want flowered ones!"

"Of course you do." Aurora rolled her eyes, her smile an indulgent one.

"Hey there, kid. Got a hug for your uncle?" Harrison asked.

She smiled up at him and wrapped her thin arms around his neck. "Guess what?" she yelled in his ear. "My tooth is loose!" She leaned back and wiggled her bottom front tooth.

Harrison juggled her easily. "Very cool. Now give me a kiss."

She smacked her lips on his cheek. Then, as if an idea hit her, she braced her hands on his cheeks. "Can we do it, Uncle Harrison? Please?"

Winter didn't know what *it* was but from the others' laughter, they did.

Harrison narrowed his gaze and appeared deep in thought. "Well, I don't know…"

"Please!"

"Okay." He shifted her higher and settled her in a sitting position on his arm so she had a higher view of the room.

Nick grabbed the nearest item, a tall candlestick, and handed it to his daughter.

She grasped the item in her hand and looked around the room. "Thank you, everyone. Thank you. I'd like to thank the Academy," Leah said, pronouncing the word properly, as she leaned forward, taking a bow.

She received a standing ovation and Winter joined in.

When the Leah show was over, Harrison lowered her to the floor and the little girl took another bow.

"Oh my God, she is adorable," Winter said in his ear.

"That child is precocious. I can't imagine her sharing the spotlight with the two babies on their way," he said of Aurora and Jade.

He seemed to catch himself and turned to face her, his expression softer than she'd ever seen it. "Make that three babies," he said, placing a hand on Winter's flat belly.

Their gazes met and held, something warm and meaningful passing between them.

"So, what's the news?" a male voice asked, breaking the spell between them.

Leah caught sight of Panda and shrieked. "Puppy!"

"Her name is Panda," Winter said, and the little girl kneeled down, her attention taken by the dog.

Michael cleared his throat. "I'll let Serenity tell you since she's been dying to spill the news," Michael said.

Winter let her gaze linger on Harrison's father, who showed what he might look like when he aged. He was a very handsome and distinguished-looking man, she mused just as his stepmom clapped her hands and Winter looked at her.

"Okay, well, here goes. We want to buy a house in the Hamptons! We want everyone to have a place to come and stay. Harrison is generous with his home, and I know Asher and Nikki will be as well, but we know life is changing, too. Especially Harrison and Winter's." Her gaze came to rest on them before she continued. "You two deserve your privacy."

Shock rippled through Winter at Serenity's words. Though a part of her wanted to object that she, Winter, had nothing to do with this large, giving family, Harrison clamped an arm around her waist as if he knew she was ready to bolt. Again. She just might have.

"We were going to look around this weekend but the realtor, a friend of Linc Kingston's, called us early this morning. A house is about to go on the market he thinks would be perfect for our family," Michael said.

Which explained their unexpected arrival.

"It has ten bedrooms, so it will cover the kids who can share if a lot of us are here at the same time," Serenity jumped in, her excitement obvious. "The realtor said we could see the place before he lists it, and we're meeting him at four p.m. today."

Michael glanced at the watch on his wrist. "Which is in twenty minutes."

Murmurs of excitement followed, Harrison's siblings talking among themselves.

"That's great," Harrison said. "Not that you aren't all welcome here but—"

"Don't worry." Serenity walked over and patted his cheek. "I booked hotel rooms for everyone from tonight through Sunday," she said with a laugh. "In case you thought we were really invading your space and your privacy."

"Oh, thank God," he muttered, and Winter couldn't help but elbow him in the side.

"That's rude!" she hissed at him.

"Oh, please. Tell me you weren't thinking the same thing."

Once again, she felt her cheeks heat, an all-too-common occurrence around Harrison and his family.

After a few more minutes, Serenity and Michael left to visit with the realtor and see the potential house, but only after they all agreed to meet in town for dinner at eight p.m.

Winter didn't miss the look between Zach and Harrison. She could practically read Harrison's mind as he silently asked his brother if she would be safe. Zach had tipped his head toward the front of the house where she knew her security guard was stationed. No doubt, she'd have company in town and that was fine with her. She wondered if coming here would diffuse the problem and hoped so.

Before she could ponder for too long, Aurora and Nick said they wanted to take Leah to the hotel so she could rest after the long ride. Jade and Knox opted to do the same, and Zach went along to hang out with his brothers at the bar while the women and Leah napped. And though Nikki offered to stay with Winter, she and Asher ended up leaving, too. Winter figured Asher had been responsible for that choice.

Harrison locked the door behind the last of their guests and turned to Winter. "Finally."

She laughed. "You're so bad."

He smiled, showing his dimples. "I love my family, but I am glad they left." He walked toward her and grasped her hand. "So how was *your* day?"

"Once I got over myself?" She shrugged. "I had a lot of fun. You're very fortunate, you know?"

He nodded. "As much as I'd often like to throttle them all, I do know that I'm lucky. My brothers and I are close. Jade too but... you know what I mean."

She laughed. "It's a guy thing. I get it."

"What did you and the girls talk about when we were huddled together discussing sports and shit?"

"Baby stuff." Her body stiffened at the reminder of the conversation. "As in how many things you need for one small infant." The women had overwhelmed her with the lists on their phones and discussion about nurseries, gliders instead of rocking chairs, and something about a Diaper Genie. Winter had no idea what that item was. But she no longer thought her apartment was large enough, and she had no idea what she should do.

Harrison squeezed her hand. "Don't worry. We'll figure it out together," he assured her.

She managed a smile, but the fact remained, she'd be alone most of the time with their baby.

"Are you sure you're up to meeting so late tonight for dinner? Because we can skip it," he offered, unaware of her panicked thoughts.

She shook her head. "I'll be fine. We can relax before then, right?"

"Of course. Want to watch a movie?" he asked.

"In that big media room?" With the couch that was perfect for sex, something she knew from experience, she mused.

He nodded, his eyes darkening with what she hoped were similar memories.

"Definitely," she said.

Tugging her along, he led them to the room at the far end of the house. They stepped inside and she glanced at the seating options that hadn't changed. Individual recliners or the massive sofa with oversized ottomans. She picked *the* couch where they could lie together, and she eased onto the cushions.

"Good choice. I'll join you in a minute," he said, his gaze watching steadily as she stretched herself out. "What movie do you want to watch?"

"One of yours?" she asked.

He shook his head. "That's a no."

She raised an eyebrow, surprised. She enjoyed his movies. He wasn't just hot man meat. He was a talented actor, able to show a wide range of emotion. "Why not?"

"Because I can't have sex with you while I'm on the large screen in front of us. Or listening to myself talk."

Her pussy clenched at his words. "You think we're going to have sex?" She was teasing him. She had every intention of getting lost in him, and whatever movie they chose didn't matter in the least.

"Damn straight, beautiful girl. Now pick."

She laughed. "Okay, how about *Die Hard?*"

"It's not Christmas," he said.

She groaned. "I'm not having the 'is it or isn't it a Christmas movie' argument." They negotiated, each suggesting a title until they finally agreed on an action adventure.

A few minutes later, he'd joined her on the couch, lounging beside her. He pulled her against him and wrapped one arm around her. She sighed and let her head rest against him. As always, when he was near comfort warred with arousal but before anything turned hot between them, she had something on her mind.

Something she'd been thinking about after watching his family dynamic. "Harrison?" She pushed herself up and they shifted so she faced him.

"What is it?" he asked.

"It's just that watching you and your family got me thinking."

"About?"

She twisted her hands together, her nerves obvious. "I think I want to get to know my father. The senator."

"I know who your father is," he said with a low chuckle. "Listen carefully." His voice turned deeper and more serious. "Getting to know the man isn't something to be scared of. You're an adult and you can call the shots. When you see him, where you get together. And I truly believe he's learned from the past. He won't be repeating the same mistakes with you that he made with Nikki."

And that was the crux of the problem, Winter thought. "But he allowed his wife, Nikki's *mother,* to treat her so cruelly. He even followed her lead."

"He did." Harrison nodded. "But he also admitted he was weak. I'm not saying he's suddenly a paragon of strength and virtue, but he has taken steps to be his own man. You've obviously seen that. Now you just need to decide if you're willing to try with him."

She pulled her bottom lip between her teeth and released it. "What if Nikki's upset about my decision?"

Reaching out, he ran his knuckles down her cheek. "Look, from what I know of your sister, she wouldn't begrudge you getting to know your father. And if he continues on the path he's been on, I believe she'll come around, too. In time."

She perked up at the thought. "I hope so. Then we'd be more of a family." She'd have a father and siblings and, dare she hope, holiday dinners? She shook her head, knowing she was getting ahead of herself.

The movie had begun, and she nudged him.

"Come on. Let's watch." Everything else would sort itself out in time.

When Harrison had suggested this movie and Winter had agreed, she'd forgotten about the steamy love scene at the end. So now she lay in the arms of a man she wanted more than words could express. And she was supposedly a woman of words. At least, that was her career.

Her sex was heavy, and need pulsed inside her just as the credits began to roll and Winter sighed. "That was amazing." Despite the need thrumming through her body, she still appreciated both the movie and the love scene she'd just watched.

"So now's not the time to tell you how clinical the actual filming is?"

She reached out, cupped her hand over the bulge in his pants and wrapped her fingers around his hard length. "This doesn't feel clinical to me," she murmured in a husky voice. In fact, there was nothing cold about the erection throbbing against her hand.

"That has nothing to do with the movie and everything to do with *you*." He dipped his head, and she felt him breathe in her hair. "You smell so damn good. Like the beach and sunshine and everything I need."

He thrust his hand into her hair and pulled her toward him, sealing his lips over hers. One slick of his tongue across her bottom lip and she let him in with a moan. He kissed her for a long time, his lips gliding over hers, devouring her mouth and taking possession.

She wanted everything he offered and helped as he slid her down, pressing her into the cushions, and grinding his jean-covered cock into her pussy. Sparks flew behind and in front of her eyes and she pulled at his shirt. "I need to feel your skin against mine," she said, desperation clawing at her.

With a nod, he rose to his feet. He stripped off his clothes and she watched his every move. Once he was undressed, her gaze came to rest on the hard, rigid cock she'd just felt against her hand.

His hot stare never leaving hers, he wrapped his fingers around the base and pumped up and down until a white bead of pre-come pooled on the head.

"Oh, God." She crawled toward him and as soon as she got close, she licked him once, then wrapped her lips around his velvety length.

He shoved his hands in her hair and held still, letting her suck him deep. She shut her eyes and reveled in the hard tug of her hair as his fingers pulled at the long strands.

Suddenly, he slid out of her mouth, leaving her bereft. "What? Why?"

He slid his hands under her arms and set her down on her knees. "You do not want this to be over that fast." He lifted her shirt, revealing her bare skin to his gaze. "Besides, you said you needed to feel skin against skin."

Dipping his head, he ran his lips over every inch of her bare flesh, tormenting her with licks of his tongue and nips of his teeth. All the while, undressing her until at last, she was naked, too.

"Lie back, beautiful."

She complied, sprawling onto her back. He placed one knee on the sofa and pulled himself up, straddling her hips and lowering himself until his cock rubbed over her sensitive sex.

"Harrison," she said on a shaky groan. "Either these pregnancy hormones are making me crazy or you're just that good. Either way, I need you inside me, *now*."

"I need you too." Still on his knees, he raised her legs and plunged into her.

"Harrison!" she cried out, arching her hips to take all of him.

He stilled, proving the man was a master at savoring moments. When they were together this summer, despite the beginnings of an emotional connection, they'd both thrown themselves into the fun side. But he was doing everything he could now to show her she meant something to him. And even she had to admit he wasn't just trying to breach the walls around her heart, he'd already climbed over.

Something she'd work through when he wasn't buried so deep inside her. He slid his large cock out of her slowly before gliding back in an equally unhurried pace. A lump rose in her throat and she fought back the tears that were building. Ones she'd never experienced during sex. There were feelings that threatened to overwhelm her as he dragged out his cock until she was empty and worked his way back in, filling her completely.

Unable to withstand the onslaught, she closed her eyes against the warmth of emotions in his expression. The sweetness in his gaze.

"Uh-uh. I want those beautiful eyes on me."

Swallowing hard, she forced her lids back open and saw the approval in the sexy lift of his lips.

"That's it, Winter. Now milk my cock."

He'd obviously made his point because as soon as she raised her hips to take him, he began to pump into her, joining their bodies in the most brutal yet necessary way. Hot sensations ripped through her, and she clenched her inner walls as her climax hit hard and she came, screaming his name.

He stiffened above her and joined her on the glorious ride.

HARRISON SAT IN his chair at the small bistro, glad it was off-season in the Hamptons. Although his family had taken over the private room in the back, the entire restaurant was on the quieter side, making the night more relaxing for everyone. The year-rounders were used to famous people buying and living here but during the summer, the tourists and visitors were more likely to gawk and not give them privacy.

His parents had put an offer on the house they'd seen this afternoon and it had quickly been accepted, so tonight wasn't just a get-together but also a celebration.

Dinner had long since finished and everyone was talking in smaller groups. He took in the family scene and let the warmth wash over him, grateful for the people in his life. Despite the rocky start he and his older siblings had thanks to their mother's mental illness, they'd managed to thrive. He'd always miss the idea of his mother, but he chose not to push to remember details because when he did, he recalled the neglect more than anything else. Until Serenity had arrived.

But here they were all together years later, and things were good. Even better now that he had Winter in his life.

Earlier, she'd had a revelation about wanting a relationship with her father, but he'd already had his own epiphany, one that was cemented tonight as he watched Winter relax around his family. She fit. As overwhelmed as she'd started out, she yearned for the closeness his siblings and parents shared, and they were all too happy to give it to her. Because his family had figured out what Harrison had been holding inside.

He loved this woman.

She had a journey of her own to complete before she could accept what was in front of her, but he intended to be by her side every step of the way. Because she loved him too. Whether she knew it or not.

He'd watched her face as he entered her, held her gaze as she found release, and saw when she'd accepted the love he showed her with both his body and his heart. But she was still skittish and often wary, like when she'd rushed off to walk Panda after they'd left the media room because their emotional connection had obviously spooked her.

And again when they'd walked into the restaurant when she'd been stiff and uncertain of her welcome. Until his sister and Aurora insisted she sit beside them. They'd pulled Winter into their circle, and he saw her visibly relax more as the evening went on.

"She looks calmer," Asher noted, picking up his glass of Dirty Dare Bourbon and taking a sip. He'd obviously caught Harrison watching Winter, who was drinking an iced tea and laughing with Nikki, Jade, and Aurora.

"She is. It's going to take time for her to realize once we let people in, we don't let them go."

Asher chuckled. "True."

Harrison glanced at his oldest brother. "Winter wants to get to know the senator, but she's worried about how Nikki will handle it." He studied Asher, who knew his fiancée better than anyone. "I told her Nikki would understand. Was I right?"

Asher sighed then nodded. "It won't be easy, but Nikki misses having her own family and her father's been trying. He's called and texted." After finishing his drink, he slid the glass away. "The senator gives Nikki space but at the same time he shows her he's not giving up. She'll be okay. I'll make sure of it."

Harrison nodded. "I figured as much."

His brother leaned an elbow on the table. "What's going on with you? It wasn't that long ago you were freaking out and drinking because she was pregnant. Now you can't take your eyes off her." Asher tipped his head toward Winter.

He wasn't wrong. Harrison squeezed the back of his neck, kneading the tight muscles there. "I think I knew the moment I laid eyes on her that she was the one."

And if he hadn't known it then, he sure as hell had the minute he'd found his way into her body. Gotten to know and admire her intelligence and saw how she'd handled announcing her relationship to Nikki and Derek and confronted the senator and his wife.

"Was it the same with you and Nikki?" he asked.

"Oh hell, no." Asher shook his head. "I saw a gorgeous, too-young for me, spoiled woman. Then I learned I was wrong about the spoiled part. And then I was fucked." He paused. "In the best possible way."

"Okay, so I was close." Harrison chuckled. "But you're right. The pregnancy did scare the shit out of me at first because I didn't see it coming. When I got my head out of my ass, I realized fate was handing me what I wanted all along."

"I'm happy for you," Asher said. "How long are you staying out here? Until the asshole is caught?"

Harrison pulled in a long breath. "It's only been one day. I need to see what Zach comes up with. He's working on it with Remy. His partner was a dick and isn't taking things seriously. But I trust Zach to figure out who's behind the threats."

"Hello," Zach said, pulling over an empty chair from the table behind them. "Did I hear my name?" He peeled off his leather jacket and hung it over the back of his chair.

"Hey," Harrison said.

"What's up?" Asher asked.

"I was thinking. Mom and Dad are buying a house here. You already have a place." He glanced at Harrison. "What if I open a second location of The Back Door?"

"I love that idea," Asher said. "Need an investor?"

"I'm pretty sure most of us would invest in anything you needed," Harrison added. "Except I don't think you need us, do you?"

Zach tipped his head. "Need and want are two different things. I am grateful for the offer. Let me think about it and get back to you."

"In the meantime, tell us what you have planned." Asher stretched an arm out and happened to reach around Nikki and hold her at the same time.

Harrison grinned, and they both listened to Zach's ideas for another establishment, this one in a luxurious summer vacation spot.

During the conversation, he glanced over and saw Winter watching him, the same way he'd been keeping an eye on her.

He met her gaze and winked.

She blushed, and he couldn't wait to get her back home and into his bed.

Chapter Twelve

ONE WEEK PASSED since Winter and Harrison had arrived at the Hamptons and she was going stir-crazy. Oh, she enjoyed his house, walking the gated property in the cool fall air, and the ability to let Panda out alone in the yard. She also appreciated the time she and Harrison spent together. They worked side by side or in nearby rooms, her on her laptop on FaceTime or Zoom interviews, and writing, and him reading scripts or meeting with Sasha, Xander, and Cassidy in person or also via video chat.

And she loved the evenings spent cooking—well, reheating meals in his kitchen—and getting to know one another better, followed by nights in his arms. A girl could get spoiled by the amount of time and attention he was giving her, and she couldn't complain. She was no longer thinking he was with her for the baby's sake. That would make no sense, given all he was doing to keep her safe and the way he looked at her. Like she belonged in this house and in his life.

She'd liked what she'd seen of the town, too—the only time she'd been allowed to visit, which was the night of the family dinner one week ago. She desperately needed a change of scenery and some time out of the house.

She knew Harrison was tied up with lawyers this morning and had taken the call in his office, so she waited until he opened the door, just before lunchtime. He stepped out and practically ran into her.

He grasped her arms. "What's wrong that you're stalking the door?" he asked. "You could have just come in."

"I didn't want to interrupt, but I was waiting for you to finish your calls. I'm going stir-crazy, Harrison. I need to get out of here for a little while. Can we go into town for lunch? Please?"

He groaned and she saw the hesitancy in his gaze.

"Pretty please? It's been quiet. Even Zach said he can't find any evidence pointing to who this person is and they haven't sent anything else to my apartment in the city. We'll take Morgan but I really need fresh air and a change of scenery." She clasped her hands together in a praying gesture.

He shook his head, placing his hands on her shoulders. "I just want to keep you safe."

"I know, and I'm grateful. But if you're with me and Morgan comes, I'll be protected. Just a quick lunch and we can walk around town for a little while. That's it."

"Fine. If Morgan's comfortable with going out,

then we can go."

She squealed her excitement and wrapped her arms around his neck in a hug. "Thank you." She breathed in his heady, masculine scent and forced herself to release her hold and step back or she wouldn't be leaving this house today.

Since she had no intention of letting Morgan talk them out of going, she rushed to the bedroom to freshen up, then walked to the kitchen to retrieve Panda's leash. She hooked her collar into the lead and met up with Harrison outside, talking to her ever-present bodyguard.

"Hello, Ms.—"

She held up a hand.

"Hello, Winter." He was a big, burly man she estimated to be around thirty years old with a full beard and a perpetual scowl that no doubt helped keep people away.

"Hi, Morgan. I'm ready."

Harrison frowned at her. "It never dawned on you that he'd say no?"

She clasped her hands in front of her. "I can be very persuasive when I want to be."

"I'm sorry, but no dog," Morgan said. "I don't want to be distracted on the off chance something happens."

"Okay." She sighed but knew if she argued, she'd

lose her opportunity.

"While you take her back inside, I'll call into the office and we'll be on our way," Morgan said, taking a few steps away.

"Sorry, buddy." She took Panda inside and checked her water before meeting Harrison back on the front porch.

He stood, arms crossed, a glare on his handsome face.

Winter rose onto her tiptoes and kissed Harrison's cheek. "Thank you," she said in an attempt to soften him up. "I'm used to the city and walking everywhere. It will feel good to have even an hour outside at a restaurant and inside some shops." She didn't even want to buy anything. She just wanted to feel free.

He groaned. "You make it hard to say no to you."

"All set," Morgan said, sliding his cell into his pocket and stepping back to them.

"Stick close," Harrison told the security guard. "Just because *he's* okay with us going to town because it's been so quiet doesn't mean I'm comfortable with it." That comment was for her, and she knew it.

"I understand." When they'd been with his family, they'd been dropped at the door and escorted right back out again. "We'll be back here before you know it."

Morgan drove his black SUV into town, finding a

parking spot on a side road off the main strip of shops, close to the café where she wanted to eat. The weather was cool on the water, and she wore a light jacket with a pair of jeans, a long-sleeve thermal top, and a fun scarf she'd wrapped around her neck.

As soon as they met on the sidewalk, Harrison slid his hand into hers and they began to walk, Morgan silently close behind.

"I really do love it here," she said, not wanting Harrison to think it was the Hamptons she didn't enjoy. "It's just been hard being cooped up."

He squeezed her hand tighter. "I understand and I hate the fact that me being famous has any impact on you at all or puts you or our baby at risk."

"I don't blame you," she murmured. "I've interviewed a lot of famous people and it's something that comes with the territory, unfortunately."

"Wait. A bookstore." He came to a stop in front of a Ye Old Books.

"Do you want something to read?" she asked.

"Yes." He turned to her, sliding his hands inside her jacket and holding her around the waist. "A baby book." His cheeks turned a ruddy shade of red, and his embarrassment stole the last piece of her heart.

"That's the sweetest thing," she said, her gaze holding his.

"I can't share this with you if I don't know what's

happening or what to expect."

God, he was going to make an amazing father, and she was beginning to believe a reliable partner, too. She didn't know what fate had in store but suddenly she had more hope.

He kissed her forehead and she sighed with pleasure.

Releasing her, he stepped back, and she swayed, unexpectedly dizzy. She reached out and grabbed onto his arm for support.

"Are you okay?" he asked.

"Yes. Sorry. I haven't eaten anything since breakfast."

He scowled and grasped her hand, pulling her against him.

"I didn't want to interrupt your meetings, and I had hoped you'd say yes so, I waited for you to be finished. I wasn't hungry when we left the house," she assured him.

His frown never wavered as he held onto her, leading her past the bookstore and to the nearest café. Tables sat empty outside, and he made sure she was sitting before he glanced at Morgan.

"I'm getting her something to eat. Keep an eye on her." Harrison bent down and explained, "Normally he'd sit a table away and keep an eye from there, but I want him right by your side."

The other man nodded and stepped closer to her chair.

Understanding Harrison's concern, she didn't utter a word of complaint.

"Do you know what you want to eat, or should I get you a menu?" he asked.

"Nikki said the chocolate chip pancakes here are to die for. She deprived herself for so long when she modeled, she's been tasting everything she's ever wanted. And she's had these twice when they've come to check on the house."

Harrison laughed. "Pancakes it is."

He shot Morgan a warning glance, pulled open the door, and walked inside. Following him with her gaze, she glanced in the window and was surprised to see a line of customers at the counter.

Prepared to wait, she crossed one leg over her other thigh and looked behind her to Morgan. "Can you sit and talk, or would that be violating some kind of bodyguard rule?"

His lips twitched, and she sensed how much he wanted to chuckle.

"It's fine. I won't tell if you crack a smile." She glanced around the mostly empty sidewalks. "And I don't think anyone will notice if you do."

He shook his head. "I'll stand on the other side so you don't have to crane your neck to talk to me."

He stepped around her and settled with his back against the plate glass window, his eagle eyes hidden behind sunglasses, but she had faith there was nothing and nobody he'd miss.

"You know I'm a journalist—reporter, right?" she asked.

He inclined his head. "I've read the file on you."

She wrinkled her nose. "I didn't consider that you needed background on me, too, when it comes to protecting us and figuring out who's behind it. Did you find out anything interesting? Besides the things the whole world now knows about," she muttered.

Which reminded her. She pulled out her phone to call her fath—the senator after she was done talking to Morgan.

"All standard background info," Morgan assured her. His head turned, following the path of a Mercedes that drove down the street, its reflection obvious in the window of the restaurant.

"Well, I would love to talk to you about your job. I was thinking of sitting down with Dana to start because I want the article to be female-centric, but you could give me a rundown on what you do."

"When I don't have to focus on the job," he told her.

Which she took to mean he wasn't going to spill. That was fine. She'd call Dana and see if she was interested in being an anonymous source.

For now, Winter turned her attention back to the senator and pulled up the number she'd saved, her finger hovering over his name. If she wanted to have a relationship with the man, she needed to reach out and try.

She bit down on the inside of her cheek, hesitating. She hadn't discussed things with Nikki and needed to talk to her sister first.

She tapped on her favorites from the screen.

"I don't like this," Morgan said, his clipped tone capturing her attention.

"What's wrong?" She glanced up at him.

He adjusted his silver-framed sunglasses. "Same vehicle has gone by here three times, slowing down when they pass. I need to get you out of here."

She shook her head. "Harrison's inside. He'll panic if we aren't here when he comes out."

She tried to pull up his cell phone number instead of Nikki's, but her hands were trembling, even as she told herself Morgan was just being proactive and doing his job. That there was nothing to worry about.

"And he'll be furious if something happens, and I didn't act." Morgan grasped her elbow and helped her to her feet, turning her toward where they'd parked the SUV and started to haul her in that direction.

"What's going on?" she asked.

"Call it gut instinct."

Everything after that happened in slow motion.

A dark Mercedes turned the corner from that same street, and Morgan jerked her to a halt. "Head inside the store," he bit out, obviously intent on getting her to safety. From what, she didn't understand, because the car was driving down the street that ran parallel to the store. But she wasn't about to make his job difficult, and she turned to the café.

The front entrance was a few feet away. She took two steps back the way she'd come when screeching tires sounded from behind her. Suddenly, Morgan shoved her with all his strength. She screamed and her head hit the metal surrounding the glass window with a sickening, painful thud.

HARRISON HADN'T WANTED to take this trip into town in the worst way, and as he waited in line, his nerves increased. If Winter hadn't been hungry to the point where she was dizzy, he'd walk out and head straight home. But he couldn't pinpoint a good reason for his anxiety. He'd taken Winter into town with his family and one security guard, and he hadn't been overly concerned. But a week had passed with no more threatening deliveries and Zach hadn't been able to figure out who'd sent the ultrasound with the dire warning.

It felt like the person was lying in wait and biding their time. Remy's partner still insisted Harrison was overreacting and though Morgan's boss believed in safety protocols, even he wondered if they were dealing with a nut job who might not act again. But Harrison's gut churned anyway. He felt safe at home. Everything about Winter being in public and exposed felt wrong.

Even knowing he was going to upset her, he ordered the meal to go and watched through the window as she talked to Morgan. Harrison kept an eye on her from inside and he had her security guard right there.

"Harrison Dare?" a female voice called his name.

Shit, he thought. The last thing he wanted to do was be recognized now. Still, he lived here, and his reputation was important to him. He didn't need his family suffering because word got around Harrison Dare treated people like a rude asshole.

Clenching his teeth, he turned around and began the small talk expected of him as he signed autographs for a woman who had four daughters and eight grandchildren.

Finally, the server behind the counter called his name, not his real one because who needed *that* announced out loud?

Harrison met the woman's gaze and treated her to his patented smile. "I hope this is all good, ma'am. I need to get food for my pregnant girlfriend. I'm sure you understand."

Her grin told him she read the tabloids. "Just one picture first? Please?"

Forcing himself to keep his smile, he stepped beside her, his back to the entrance. A loud screech had him jerking in time to see a vehicle turn and come straight toward the front windows.

"Move!" Harrison yelled at the female fan, pushing her aside and running for Winter.

He heard the shouts and panicked yelling of people around him as the car shattered the window in front of where Winter had been sitting seconds before. Glass flew and people screamed as the car came to a stop halfway through the store. Harrison didn't see anyone pinned by the car and someone else could check on the driver. His sole focus had to be Winter.

He rushed to find her outside. The door wasn't damaged, and he yanked it open and stepped out. He looked around, finding her and Morgan immediately. The bodyguard lay on the sidewalk groaning in pain, his leg at an odd angle as he dragged his body toward Winter, who lay unmoving on the ground.

"Winter!" Harrison rushed over and kneeled down at her side. Blood trickled down her temple from where she'd hit her head and her hair was matted with the brown substance. And she was unconscious.

"Someone call 9-1-1!" he yelled, his heart pounding so hard it threatened to beat out of his chest.

"I already did," a female voice said from behind him.

"Morgan!" Harrison barked out without taking his gaze from Winter's pale face. "You okay?"

"Leg's probably broken," the man said through obvious agony. "I saw the car turn directly toward her and I pushed her out of the way. She hit her head, dammit. I saw that car drive by a few times. It was suspicious, and I was getting her out of there, but I was too late."

Harrison heard his groan. "You did the right thing," he said, glancing over his shoulder at the bodyguard.

Sweat beaded on the man's forehead and pain was etched all over his face. Behind him, people swarmed the car. The driver's side door had been flung open, and the airbag had deployed and was visible, but Harrison didn't see the driver. Who, it *seemed*, had deliberately targeted Winter.

When an older woman kneeled by Morgan's side, taking care of him, Harrison turned back to focus on Winter.

He stroked her soft cheek, ignoring the people that

were surrounding them and gawking. "Come on, beautiful. Open those pretty green eyes." *Please*, he thought, silently begging.

Sirens sounded from a distance, the noise growing louder as the ambulance approached. The vehicle screeched to a halt and a police car quickly joined it. The paramedics rushed over to Winter and Morgan. Harrison wasn't certain if anyone else had been injured.

"Excuse me, sir." One of the paramedics pushed him out of the way.

"She's pregnant," Harrison told the man.

"Got it."

Harrison stood by uselessly and watched, unable to do a damned thing for the woman he loved. Another paramedic joined the first, and together they worked to stabilize Winter's neck before moving her to a stretcher.

All the while, Harrison's stomach churned, panic pulsing inside him. The ambulance could only hold one person, and they already had more on the way for Morgan and whoever needed help. An unconscious Winter had been triaged and taken first.

Harrison was vaguely aware of the police swarming the vehicle that'd caused the incident. Despite Morgan's certainty that the crash had been intentional, Harrison couldn't split his focus. It had been difficult when worrying about both the bodyguard and Winter, but the other man had been injured on the job. He'd undertaken the risk.

Winter needed him more.

Once the medics loaded the stretcher into the back of the vehicle, Harrison stepped up. "I want to ride with you." He braced a hand on the side of the truck's open back end.

"Mr. Dare—" It was obvious the man recognized him.

"She's my fiancée and her only family is a couple of hours away. Please."

The two medical personnel shot each other looks and one nodded. "Front passenger seat. Let's go."

Relieved, Harrison rushed to the front of the ambulance, flung open the door, and climbed in. On the drive to the hospital, he texted his family group chat, filling them in. He called Asher with more detail so his brother could break the news to Nikki. And Harrison asked Asher to make sure she got word to Derek and the senator. To Winter's family: the one she wanted to create for herself, and the one Harrison wanted her to be part of.

He braced a hand on the back seat and attempted to turn but a wall blocked him from seeing Winter.

"Stay calm," the driver said. "We don't know anything yet."

Harrison nodded at the man who had no doubt seen his share of worried family members. "Thanks."

A few minutes later, the ambulance pulled into the bay at the hospital and Harrison was forced into a jam-packed waiting room to pace while they took Winter to assess her injuries and run tests. Considering it was off-season, the amount of sick and hurt people coming through surprised him.

After an hour, he was losing his mind. He asked professionals who walked through the doors if they could check on Winter and they all explained the emergency room was busy and he needed to wait. Someone would come to talk to him. He tried asking about Morgan too but given how annoying he'd already been, he received more grunts than actual replies.

He lowered himself into a chair with a groan and laced his fingers together, raising his arms and clasping his hands behind his neck and pulling on his tight muscles. It didn't help relax him.

People came and went around him, and another hour passed. Though he wanted to throw his famous weight around, nothing would get him answers until the doctors had some themselves.

"Harrison!" Nikki's voice brought him out of his stupor. He rose to his feet, and she barreled into him, wrapping her arms around him tight.

He hugged her back and met his brother's gaze over her head. "Did you break speeding records getting here?"

Asher shrugged. "Whatever it takes."

"What do you know? How is she? It's been hours and I know I'd have heard from you if you had good news." Nikki shot questions at him.

"I don't know." He curled his hands into fists, his frustration at an all-time high. "Nobody will tell me a damned thing. I've asked every medical professional who walks through those doors to get me answers. They just keep saying they're backed up and someone will come talk to me soon. And I pulled the fiancé card," he warned Nikki.

She gasped. "Are you——?"

"Not yet," he muttered. But he'd be locking Winter down as soon as he could. Maybe it was too soon but he didn't care.

He *knew* she was his.

Her sister blew out a long breath. "Since we have time, what exactly happened?"

"I swear to fuck, I don't know." Harrison ran a hand through his already disheveled hair. He'd been shoving his fingers through it all day. "Winter was going stir-crazy and begged me to go into town for lunch and to walk around. Since the bodyguard agreed, we went. But I was uneasy." He shook his head, regretting the entire day.

Asher placed a calming hand on his shoulder. "Breathe," he commanded.

Harrison inclined his head and inhaled, then let out a long exhale before meeting Nikki's gaze. "Winter was dizzy and hadn't eaten, so I left her sitting at an outside table at the café with the bodyguard and I went inside. I fucking ordered the food *to go* because I had a bad feeling. Next thing I know, a car's tires are screeching, and a vehicle is headed directly for where Winter was sitting. It crashed into the café window and came to a grinding stop."

Asher let out a low whistle. "Damn."

"It happened in seconds," Harrison said. "The car crashed into the glass, and I ran to find Winter. Morgan had been hit and his leg is probably broken. And Winter was on the ground, unconscious."

Nikki closed her eyes and moaned.

Though he'd already told them Winter had suffered a head injury, hearing the details couldn't be easy and Asher enfolded Nikki in his arms.

"Family of Winter Capwell?" A woman wearing scrubs stood by the doors Harrison had been watching for hours.

"Here," Nikki said before he did. She broke free from Asher, and they all stepped toward the doctor.

"I'm Dr. Kline. I've been treating Winter." Despite

the doctor's severe appearance, her dark hair pulled back in a tight bun, she smiled in a way obviously meant to reassure them. "She's conscious now. I thought I should lead with that."

"Oh, thank God," Nikki blinked as big crocodile tears fell from her eyes.

Harrison nodded, the lump in his throat massive. "What else?" he managed to ask.

"She has a severe concussion. It's grade three, meaning she lost consciousness. As I said, she's awake, and she'll be fine in time."

"The baby?" he asked, holding his breath.

"Also fine."

He expelled air and hoped he didn't pass out. "Okay, good. Good."

Asher gripped Harrison's shoulder in one hand and held onto Nikki with the other.

"Before you see her," the doctor continued, "you should be aware of some of her symptoms. Aside from the obvious pain she is in, she's extremely dizzy and nauseous, and she has no memory of the accident—which is common for a concussion as severe as hers. But I do expect those memories to return."

Harrison was nauseous himself. "Go on."

"There are other, less severe symptoms, and I'll give you a list of what to watch for when we discharge her. But we've done a CT scan and she has no swelling, bleeding of the brain or a skull fracture, which is excellent news." The doctor held her clipboard against her chest.

"Oh my God." Nikki's knees almost buckled and Asher held her upright. She probably just now realized how bad this could have been.

The woman shot Nikki a sympathetic glance. "Given that she lost consciousness, I'd like to keep her overnight for observation. If nothing changes, she can go home tomorrow."

Harrison let out yet another relieved breath, knowing he'd be sitting in a chair in her room all night.

"But she will need to be watched and her symptoms can last for weeks, if not months."

"I've got her," Harrison said.

"We all do," Nikki said, and Asher nodded.

"Meanwhile, we'll keep checking her hormone levels for the baby and monitor them both."

"Thank you, Dr. Kline. When can we see her?" he asked.

"You can go in one at a time until she's settled in a room. Then it's two people max during visiting hours."

Harrison closed his eyes and when he opened them, he did the most difficult thing he could imagine. "Why don't you go in," he said to Nikki.

Her eyes opened wide. "But—"

"Go," he said gruffly. "I'll go arrange for a private room. Maybe then we can get more of us in at once. I'll switch with you as soon as I'm done."

Asher sent him a grateful look.

"Why don't you both come with me," the doctor said. "I'll send each of you in the right direction."

Harrison and Nikki followed her through the doors, and she gave him directions before continuing on with Nikki.

He waited until he had turned a corner and knew he was alone before he leaned against the wall and let himself break down. Alone.

WINTER CAME TO in the tunnel of a machine and immediately panicked. Moving hurt her eyes and her head pounded with excruciating ferocity. The technician shut down what turned out to be a CT scan to talk and calm her down. A doctor came in to reassure her that both she and the baby were okay. But Winter's anxiety increased when she couldn't remember having been in an accident. The last thing she recalled was getting into the SUV at Harrison's house to go into town.

Thanks to the doctor, who had a good bedside manner, and the patient technician, Winter managed to finish the test with tears leaking from her eyes from the combination of pain, dizziness, and nausea.

Once she'd been returned to her cubicle on a stretcher, the nurse dimmed the overhead lights, let her take acetaminophen, and told her to rest while the doctor waited for test results.

She must have fallen asleep because the next time she woke up, she felt a warm, large hand in hers. Forcing her eyelids open wasn't easy, and when the room stopped spinning, she saw Harrison's worried gaze on hers.

He looked exhausted, as if he'd aged years in the last few hours.

"Thank God you're awake." He brought her hand to his mouth and brushed his lips over her skin. "How bad do you feel?" he asked without sugar-coating things.

"Like I've been hit by a bus, but I heard it was a combination of metal and tempered glass. Not that I remember." She spoke softly to minimize the impact on her head pain, something she'd learned when interacting with the doctor and nurses.

She didn't want to talk at all because of how much any little thing hurt her head, but she had something to say. "I'm sorry, Harrison."

He blinked in confusion. "*For what?* I'm the one who's sorry anything in my life could hurt you this way." He reached a hand out to touch her head, then thought better of his actions and put his hand back on the bed.

His agonized expression broke her heart. "This isn't your fault. Every day people can end up with stalkers. Do the police think it was deliberate? Not a simple car jumping the curb and crashing into the restaurant?"

He rubbed his thumb back and forth over the top of her hand. "Morgan says—"

"Oh my God, Morgan! How is he?" She bolted upright in bed and regretted it instantly. "Oh God." She moaned and leaned back against the pillows.

"Be careful, please? Try not to move." His voice cracked as he lightly touched her cheek.

She swallowed back tears. "Tell me Morgan is okay."

Harrison nodded. "He's in surgery to set his broken leg but he should be fine once he heals."

She ran her tongue over her dry lips. "I feel awful he was injured because of me."

"Hey. He'd be the first to say he was doing his job."

"Okay. What were you going to say about him? Before I interrupted?" she asked.

He frowned. "Morgan thinks the same car drove past the café a handful of times and…" He hesitated.

"It's okay, just tell me."

"He believes the car deliberately turned your way and accelerated until the café stopped its trajectory."

She closed her eyes for a brief second. "God. This is crazy. Who wants to hurt me?"

He squeezed her hand. "We're going to find out," he promised. "Do you know or remember everything the doctors said about your injuries?"

"The baby is fine." He squeezed her hand tighter, and she managed a full smile.

"Yes," she murmured. "I remember *that*." And the relief that had swelled inside her. The peanut inside her may not have been planned, but she wanted the baby with everything in her heart.

From the relieved look on Harrison's face, he now felt the same way.

"The CT Scan results aren't back yet. And Nikki was in to visit but you were sleeping, and she didn't want to wake you. She sat for a bit while I arranged for you to be moved to a private room since they want to keep you overnight."

She was too tired to argue. "Thank you," she said groggily, suddenly wiped out. Like just talking was too much effort.

"Sleep, Winter. I asked, and the doctor said it was safe with the concussion."

Her eyelids felt heavy, and she couldn't even manage a nod. "'Kay."

She placed her free hand on her belly and let herself go, floating somewhere she was aware of the pain but didn't have to work so hard to stay focused.

"Sleep," he said again. "I've got you." His warm hand covered hers, protecting the life inside her. "I've got you both."

Then silence descended. Only the sound of footsteps and voices outside the curtain reached her ears but from a hazy distance.

"I love you," he said as she fell into a deep sleep.

Chapter Thirteen

I T WAS AFTER dinner by the time Winter was moved into a private room. Although much of his family had driven here after hearing the news, Harrison asked them to wait until tomorrow to visit. If Winter wasn't discharged before visiting hours started, they could come by. Tonight, she needed to sleep.

After a stare-down with a nurse, she allowed him to stay overnight. It helped that he offered to have his publicist send a signed movie poster for the daughter he'd heard her mention to a colleague. The couch in the room was small, but he had no intention of sleeping there.

He called his housekeeper to go to the house and feed, walk and check on Panda, but Mrs. Baker insisted on taking the dog to her house until Winter was settled back home so they didn't have to worry. And once he told Winter her dog was taken care of, she'd been able to close her eyes.

Harrison slept in a chair by Winter's side. He put his head on her mattress and kept her hand in his. The one thing he didn't do was badger Winter to talk about her ordeal or ask her questions. He was content to be with her, and there was plenty of time to talk later. Thank God.

The next morning, the doctor who needed to check Winter before she was discharged had a family emergency and was coming in later in the day. Given how much pain Winter was still in, Harrison didn't mind. He liked Dr. Kline and was comfortable with her treating Winter. Neither he nor Winter slept well. Typical of hospitals, someone came in every three to four hours to wake up Winter and do their usual medical checks.

Zach texted that he was on his way from the city to see Winter. He also said he had information and insisted on meeting with Harrison and Asher alone. Since Nikki and Derek had come to visit, he left Winter with her family and met up with Asher and Zach in the waiting room. One that was more private than the crowded emergency room had been yesterday.

Zach's brother pulled him into a one-armed hug. "Fuck. I'm sorry I didn't figure this out before Winter was hurt."

Harrison swallowed hard. "She's going to be okay. That's what matters."

Asher and Zach did their own brotherly hug.

"So, what do you know?" Harrison asked.

"And why did you need us both?" Asher folded his

arms across his chest.

Zach tipped his head toward a private corner and they sat, Zach and Asher on a sofa and Harrison in a chair pulled close to them. A television was bolted into the wall across the way, the volume on low and another couple talked quietly on the far side of the room before stepping into the hall.

But for the three of them, the room was empty.

"I hacked into the security feeds from street cameras first and then the café shop," Zach said in a low voice. "I also did some digging into what the police know, and I casually spoke to some of the witnesses."

Harrison inclined his head. "Morgan already told the police the car had passed by the café a few times, scoping out the area and he thought the driver deliberately turned and sped up, aiming at Winter."

"Based on the video and witness statements, I'd agree," Zach said. "The driver turned toward where Winter was standing and hit the gas. The car lurched forward and kept going. Morgan flung your girl out of the way and the car hit his leg."

Harrison winced. "What else?"

Asher leaned forward, listening in his quiet way.

"The license plate is registered to a man who lives in New York City. Local police are coordinating with the New York cops to bring him in for a chat. Suffice it to say, Remy's partner is taking this case more seriously now."

Harrison rolled his eyes, not in the mood for the asshole who'd minimized her fear.

"But the owner of the vehicle either lent it to the culprit or his wife did because neither of them were driving." Zach held up a hand to stop Harrison's next question. "I need to work my way to the answer. Trust me, you both need every detail." He drew a deep breath. "Witnesses saw the driver exit the vehicle. A probable female with a scarf around her head and dark sunglasses covering her eyes. She slipped away in the commotion after, but thanks to the security cams, I managed to capture her face and profile both in the car and as she left the vehicle."

"Good." Harrison blew out a breath and waited for his brother to continue. To fucking tell him who was responsible.

"I sent the feed to my friends, Adam Miles and Jacob Dean, in Dallas. They used to work for McKay-Taggart and recently opened their own company after developing high-tech software to find missing people. Miles, Dean, Weston, and Murdoch."

Asher drummed his fingers on the table. "I've heard of them. MD. Mass Destruction."

"It's MDWM," Zach said. "And the cops just like to make a joke of the name but not of the software. That shit is brilliant."

Harrison shook his head. Zach always had the right contacts in every situation.

"Didn't those guys go undercover on a movie set with Jared Johns, the actor? The feds thought he was a serial killer or something?" Asher asked.

Harrison wrinkled his forehead. "How the hell would you know that?"

"I read the news, dumbass. Besides, didn't you lose the role in that movie to Johns?" Asher asked.

"I hate when you revert to brotherly behavior," Harrison muttered. "Yes, I did. And the guy's best friend turned out to be a serial killer. Now can we get back on track?"

"Right. Well, MDWM's software has taken down a fuck ton of criminals. And they found us one more, the person driving who targeted Winter." Zach watched him and Asher warily.

Harrison stilled. "Go on. I'm assuming they identified the driver that hit Winter." His stomach twisted in knots as Zach nodded.

"They did. Now brace yourselves."

Both Harrison and Asher leaned forward.

"Collette Bettencourt was driving."

Harrison blinked, certain he'd heard wrong.

"No." Asher rose to his feet. "No fucking way. You're saying I have to tell Nikki that *her mother* tried to run over her pregnant sister?" He caught his voice rising and slung himself back into the seat. "Fuck."

"Fuck is right," Harrison muttered. "All this time we're thinking it's a crazed fan, and it's her father's wife? The same woman who paid off Winter's mother to have an abortion?"

Zach groaned. "I wish it was a sick fuck fan nobody knew."

"What did you do with the information?" Asher asked before Harrison could.

His mind was still on Winter. Asher would be formulating ways to both protect and tell Nikki.

Zach rubbed the back of his neck. "I'm sitting on it until you two tell me what the fuck you want me to do. On the one hand, Nikki and Derek are impacted. On the other, there's the former senator. And then there's Winter, the victim."

"I don't think it's fair to give them a choice," Asher said. "Asking Nikki and Derek if it's okay to turn the information over to the cops is asking their permission to lock up their mother. The senator *says* he's cut ties with his wife but none of us want him to instigate some kind of cover-up."

Harrison nodded. "Agreed. And Winter won't want to hurt her new siblings by telling you to give the cops the footage." He rose and began to pace, then came to a decision and spun back to his brothers. "Turn it over to the cops," Harrison said.

"I agree," Asher said. "It's not a decision anyone should make except those who found the evidence and that answers the question. It's evidence. Do the legal thing."

Zach blew out an obviously relieved breath. He stood and Asher followed. "Since I assumed that would be the outcome of this discussion, Remy's standing by with the video evidence. He's a detective, and he always had every intention of following the law. I just wanted to make sure you two ran through all scenarios in case I had to talk you into it. Glad I didn't have to."

Pulling his phone out of his leather jacket, Zach hit a few buttons and put the phone to his ear. "Remy? Turn it in." He listened, then said, "Yeah. Everyone's okay here. Thanks, man." Zach disconnected the call.

"You both good?" he asked.

Asher shook his head. "Fuck, no. I have to talk to Nikki and Derek before this goes public."

"And I have to tell Winter and prepare the senator." Harrison wondered if this day would ever end. "Fuck my life," he muttered as they all strode out of the room.

WINTER LAY IN the hospital bed, with Nikki and

Derek in her room trying to keep her entertained. Harrison told her that his parents had driven up early this morning and would come to visit when she was up to it. She was grateful they cared enough to drive two hours or more because she'd been injured.

When her brother and sister walked in, she tried not to break down in tears. Not just because of the pain but because they were here, and they obviously loved her, and she was so glad to have them in her life. Despite the short time she'd known them, they looked wrecked by her injuries. Nikki's eyes were red from crying, and Derek had been pacing since he arrived.

"Thank you so much for coming," Winter said, her voice still a deliberate whisper in deference to the throbbing in her skull.

Derek spun to face her and narrowed his gaze. "You're family. We wouldn't be anywhere else."

"He means that more sweetly than it came out. He's stressed and upset too," Nikki said, sitting by Winter's bedside. She tucked a strand of her long hair behind her ear.

"I know," Winter murmured.

Derek walked over to the bed and squeezed her covered foot. "So, Harrison asked me to let our father know you're here. I called, and he was upset. He said he'd be here as soon as he could."

Winter's gaze rested on Nikki's. "Please don't be

angry. I spent time with Harrison's family and they're so close. I've never had that, and I hoped maybe I could start by seeing if our father is really trying to do better."

"Oh, Winter. I could never be angry or upset with you for wanting a relationship with him. I… I miss what I didn't have. A father, a mother who cared."

Derek's hand came down on Nikki's shoulder, and she covered it with her own.

"He's been calling and texting. I just haven't been able to bring myself to get back to him. I'm scared that he'll hurt me again. I only answered my mother's call because I forgot to check who it was first."

She gave a little shrug, but Winter understood. Tears pooled in her eyes, and Nikki also sniffed and swiped at her damp cheeks.

"I swear to you all, I want to do better." The former senator stood in the doorway, obviously having overheard at least some of their conversation.

Derek turned. "Dad. You have impeccable timing. And as usual, I see the rules don't apply to you. They said two visitors. Even Harrison is abiding by them."

"My child is in here. Nobody was going to keep me away. And I'm glad you're all here together." He paused. "I'm pleased to have my children in one place."

Nikki stiffened.

Winter wanted to hug her, but she couldn't move without pain.

"I'm glad too," Winter said. "For the next few minutes, can we just be here together? We have enough issues to work out for years to come. Cut the injured one some slack, okay?" Winter knew she was asking a lot of Nikki and she'd have to make it up to her.

Nikki clasped her hand and squeezed. "Of course."

The senator pulled up an empty chair and sat down. "So… you and Harrison are still together. Is it serious?"

Clearly he had no issue prying, Winter thought. "Umm…"

"He hasn't left her side and he slept here last night. I'd say he's serious," Derek said, chuckling.

Nikki elbowed him in the ribs and Winter did her best not to laugh. Her head didn't need the pain.

The words *I love you* floated through her brain in Harrison's deep voice, but Winter couldn't be certain if he'd said them, she'd dreamed them, or was making it up completely. Her chest squeezed at the thought.

"I see your expression," the man she wasn't quite ready to call dad said. "You're serious about him."

Her eyes filled because he was right. She was very serious about Harrison. "He's been good to me, and he wants to be there for the baby." And she was still being cautious.

Given the dynamic in this room, the distrust, how could she throw herself into a relationship headfirst without watching her heart?

"I'm going to give you one piece of fatherly advice and then I'll back off. I'd give it to all three of you, but Nikki and Derek have already learned this particular lesson."

Winter waited as he appeared to gather his thoughts.

"If you love Harrison, don't let him go without being honest about your feelings or you'll spend the rest of your life filled with regrets. Like I have." He paused, then turned to face his other children. "I can't say I regret my marriage to Collette because I wouldn't have the two of you, and despite my behavior, I do love you both." He held up his hands as if to say he was finished.

A sound rose from Nikki's throat and Winter knew she was choked up.

Winter's phone rang from the counter next to her, breaking the awkward tension. The police found her cell on the ground outside the café and returned it when they came to question her last night. At least she knew it still worked.

"Just let it go to voice mail," she said.

The phone rang until it clicked off. Then Winter,

her siblings, and their father talked about benign things like the weather, Derek's latest business deal and he asked about Nikki's work with K-Talent Productions.

Despite wanting her visitors to stay, Winter yawned and winced at the motion.

"We should let you get some sleep," Nikki said, pushing herself up from the sofa where she'd sat down earlier.

Winter wanted to argue but couldn't. She needed rest.

"I'll come to visit tomorrow when you're home and settled," Nikki promised.

"I'm going to hold you to that," Winter said to her sister. "Before you go, can you check my cell and tell me who left a message? I can't see well. I'm still dizzy."

Her sister stepped over to the dresser by the bed and picked up the phone. She glanced at the screen and gasped, the color draining from her face.

"Nikki?" Derek moved beside her as she dropped the cell like it was poison.

"Who is it?" he asked, and Winter did her best to remain still while waiting for an answer.

The senator kneeled and picked up the device from the floor. Glancing down at the lit-up screen, his eyes opened wide. "It's a phone number you wouldn't know," he said to Winter. "But *we* do."

"It's Mom's number," Nikki said, her voice numb.

"Shit," Derek muttered.

Aware she wasn't firing on all cylinders and things were fuzzy, Winter couldn't figure out what was going on. "I don't understand."

"Play it," Derek ordered.

Winter had never seen him strung so tight. Not even when his ex-girlfriend had attempted to destroy Jessica's life and business. Winter didn't know why Collette would call her or how the woman had gotten her number, but the senator's wife was connected with many important people and no doubt she had her ways.

The senator swiped the phone screen. "I need to hold it up to your face for recognition," he explained.

Winter held herself still. "Go ahead."

He handled it quickly, and soon Collette's voice filled the room.

"You're a whore like your mother. You cost me my family and my husband the presidency. You should have had an abortion like your mother should have done. I won't miss hitting you next time."

Her father stared at the phone, his face twisted in shock and horror. Winter realized she'd thought of him as *her father* for the first time but couldn't focus on that now.

Blood drained from her head as the hateful words came back to her, repeating themselves on a loop in her mind. Her already aching head began to throb with a steady beat as she fought the lump in her throat and the tears that wanted to pour out. Nobody had ever talked to her with so much venom before.

"She used her own phone," Derek said, his tone rising in obvious shock.

"And she didn't even bother to try and disguise her voice," the senator spoke next as he placed her phone back on the counter. "Collette has completely lost her mind." He shook his head. "What am I talking about? She went after you in her car. Of course, she lost her mind."

Or she was just pure evil. At this point, Winter wasn't sure the distinction mattered, at least not to her.

Shaking, Nikki lowered herself to the chair, silently crying.

Every one of them sat in their own shocked world. Suddenly, Harrison rushed in, Asher behind him. Zach took up the rear.

"What happened?" Harrison strode to Winter's beside. "Did you do something to upset her?" he demanded of her father.

"Harrison, no. We… I mean, I just got a phone call. A voice mail, actually."

"Who called? What's going on?"

Winter glanced to where Asher had kneeled down by Nikki's side. They talked quietly while Derek stood with his jaw clenched.

Winter sighed, trying to form the words to explain.

"How about I just play the voice mail?" the senator asked.

Winter began to shake. "No. I don't want to hear it again."

Harrison put a hand on her arm. "Someone needs to explain. Now." He gritted his teeth, his care and concern for her obvious.

Asher rose to his feet and pulled Nikki to a standing position and curled an arm around her shoulders. Winter was so glad her sister had such a good man in her life. She'd need Asher more than ever now.

"They already know," Asher said.

"Know *what*?" Harrison bit out, his frustration clear.

Her father cleared his throat. "That my soon-to-be ex-wife tried to kill my daughter."

Harrison ran a hand over his face and looked around the room. "How do you all know it was Collette? Who was on the voice mail?" he asked.

Winter narrowed her gaze. "A better question is, why aren't the three of you surprised?"

"Zach saw footage of the incident and the video camera caught the driver's face. He had friends run it through facial recognition software. We were coming to tell you." Harrison raised an eyebrow at the senator. "Your turn."

He sighed, his shoulders drooping. "Collette called Winter while we were here. She let the call go to voice mail. We played it. My… wife, threatened Winter and the baby, and admitted what she'd done."

Harrison turned to Winter, his eyes wide. "Are you kidding me?"

She shook her head and winced, and he brushed a tear off her cheek.

"My friend, Remy, turned the video over to the police." Zach glanced around the room. "In case anyone had the inclination to hide the truth," he said, his gaze coming to rest on the senator.

The other man shook his head.

"We need to give them the voice mail, too," Derek said.

Nikki sniffed and nodded.

Winter remained silent. It wasn't *her* mother who'd put them through this agony. Although Winter had been hurt and traumatized, her half-siblings were going through their own emotional pain.

And a part of her felt responsible. "I'm sorry." Winter hadn't intended to say the words out loud. "If I'd never come here, if I hadn't told you who I am…"

"Something else would have made my mother

snap," Derek answered immediately.

Nikki pulled out of Asher's grasp, walked over to Winter and put her head on her shoulder. "You are my sister. If you never came here, I still wouldn't have a mother who loves me the way she should. I wouldn't have a father who sees what he did wrong."

From across the room, the senator drew in a sharp breath.

"And I wouldn't have you," Nikki said softly. "I love you, Winter. So don't you dare blame yourself."

Winter hugged her back, ignoring the pain in her head from the movement as emotion lodged in her throat. "I love you, too."

And she hadn't missed that Nikki had taken a step toward reconciling with their father.

Nikki cleared his throat and treated the senator to a shaky smile. As a start, Winter would take it.

"This is not okay," a female nurse said, striding into the room, her face pinched in disapproval. "The patient cannot handle this much noise and stimulation. I don't care if one of you is a famous actor who pulled strings to get a private room, and another is a United States senator. There are too many people in here." She looked around, eyeing each visitor through her narrowed gaze.

"I'm a *former* senator," her father said, somehow breaking the tension and causing Derek and Nikki to laugh. "Besides, I need to get going. I'm going to get in touch with the authorities."

The nurse nodded. "Good. I'll leave while you all say your goodbyes. But I will check back." She straightened her shoulders and walked out of the room.

The senator turned and gave Derek a fatherly hug before walking to where Asher stood protectively beside Nikki. "Winter, take care of yourself, and I'll be in touch to see how you are feeling. But… may I take your phone to turn it in to the police?"

"Not before I get a copy of that voice mail," Zach said, his distrust of the senator obvious.

Winter didn't blame him. She wasn't sure what he intended either, though she hoped he wouldn't try and protect his wife.

Zach picked up Winter's cell without asking for permission. After using her for facial recognition, he sent himself the voice mail and handed the phone to her father. "Share it with yourself and let her keep her phone."

Her father laughed uncomfortably. "I'm not sure how."

Zach sent the incriminating evidence to the senator's phone and put the device on the counter.

He smiled at Winter, then turned. "Nikki, take care, and I hope to hear from you."

Her sister's eyes widened at his use of her pre-ferred name and glistened with more tears. "Are you going to help... *her*?" Nikki asked. "Protect her from the consequences of her actions?"

He straightened his sport coat and faced Nikki. "I'm going to make sure Collette pays for what she's done. And I do want her to get the help she needs. But I am not going back to her, nor can I forgive her for everything she's deprived me of." His warm gaze came to rest on Winter. "I'm still working on forgiving myself for all I allowed to happen. Anyway, I'll talk to you all soon."

He strode out of the room without looking back.

Winter was so tired she could barely keep her eyes open.

"We'll go, too." Asher hooked his elbow through Nikki's. "We have a lot to discuss," he said, and Nikki nodded.

They said their goodbyes and walked out, leaving Winter worried about her sister. But she knew Asher would take care of her.

Zach, the only one left aside from Harrison, turned to Winter. "I'll check in soon, okay?"

"Thank you for everything you've done for me." Zach was a special human. If Collette hadn't called and given herself away, Harrison's brother would have made sure she paid for her crimes anyway. "I don't know how to repay you, but I am so grateful."

He strode over to the bed, leaned down, and gently kissed her forehead. "You're family, pretty girl. Any time you need me, I'm here." He straightened and slapped Harrison on the back. "Take care. We'll talk soon."

"Thank you." A long look passed between the brothers before Zach walked out, leaving Harrison and Winter alone.

HARRISON PULLED A chair up to Winter's bedside. One look at her still pale face and he knew there would be no discussion between them now, either.

"Are you due for medication?" he asked.

"I think so."

"Be right back."

Thirty minutes later, because nothing ever happened quickly in a hospital, a nurse arrived with Winter's pain medicine, and she took the pills. Winter swallowed them quickly and leaned back against the pillows, her eyes closing before he could urge her to rest.

And just like he had last night, Harrison grasped her hand and stayed with her.

Chapter Fourteen

WINTER LAY IN Harrison's bed, still sore and still in pain. She didn't feel well and wouldn't for a long while. The doctor had made that clear. She couldn't look at a screen or work because of dizziness, the television always sounded too loud, and she generally felt like roadkill.

Harrison took good care of her. Following the doctor's instructions, he checked on her symptoms and made sure she remained inactive, which wasn't a hardship given she couldn't do anything else. He brought ice for her head and made sure she ate despite the queasiness that never left. At this point, she couldn't distinguish between the concussion and morning sickness, and she wasn't sure it mattered.

It was the third morning after she'd been discharged from the hospital, and she'd woken up alone. Since Harrison was also on dog duty, she assumed he was feeding Panda. God, he was so good to her. Still, she wondered if he was ready for her to be well enough to go home. He hadn't once given her the feeling he wanted her gone, but she had definitely taken over his life.

A knock sounded at the open bedroom door. She looked up to see him walk into the room. Wearing a black T-shirt and a pair of gray sweatpants that rode low on his hips, the bulge of his cock was easily visible, and she couldn't help but stare.

"Eyes up here, beautiful. It's not like we can do anything about it right now."

She pretended to pout as he strode toward her, Panda prancing at his side. Her dog jumped onto the bed and cuddled at her side. She ran her hand over her soft head, grateful for her little companion.

"What's going on?" she asked as Harrison sat on the edge of the mattress.

"I have news about Collette." His tone sounded serious.

"Tell me the police found her, please." Somehow, the woman had disappeared, and Winter's only solace was knowing she was safe at Harrison's Hamptons home with the alarm set and double security guards outside.

He shook his head. "It wasn't the police. Zach and Remy tracked her down to a rental in Maryland. The company doesn't ask for licenses to check in. The police were waiting on a warrant and Zach just did his thing and called in the tip. It's like the woman didn't even try all that hard to hide."

She closed her eyes and sighed. "She does act like

she's above the law. So she's in custody?"

Harrison nodded, and all the tension in her body rushed out at once. "It's really over?" she asked, the relief filling her enormous.

"It's over."

Ignoring her body aches and pain in her head, she sat forward. He met her halfway, and she wrapped her arms around him, hugging him tight. "I'm so glad."

He pulled her into him, and she inhaled his delicious musky scent from the soap in his shower and held back a moan.

"I know we haven't talked about that day yet because I wanted to give you time to heal, but I have never been as panicked as I was when that car drove through the restaurant, right where I'd left you sitting," he said into her hair.

She sniffed back tears. "I'm sorry I begged you to go to town. I—"

"Stop. Like I said, the only one to blame is Collette."

Winter pulled back and met his gaze. "Do Nikki and Derek know their mother is in custody?"

He nodded. "And Asher was with Nikki, so don't worry. Derek is going with your father—is it okay to call him that?"

"I think so," she murmured. "I started to think of him that way in the hospital room when we were all in there together."

Harrison held her hand in his. "Good. Derek is going with your father to where she's being held to see her. He said he'll fill us in later."

"Okay. I feel so sorry for Nikki and Derek, and even for my fa-ther." She stuttered over the word, but it was getting easier to say.

"I know. You all have a lot to face depending on how Collette handles her plea."

"Yeah. But let's not worry about that now."

He nodded. "I'm glad you're open to a relationship with the senator. You deserve a parent who loves you. So does Nikki and I hope they can work things out, too."

They sat in silence and Winter thought back to that moment in her hospital room, just her and her new-found family. The advice her father gave her had resonated deeply.

Now that the situation with Collette was resolved, she had a choice to make. She could take her father's words to heart and be brave. She could tell Harrison how she felt about him, or she could say nothing, ride out this pregnancy as co-parents who occasionally sleep together, and be riddled with regret.

She looked into his handsome face and knew he was everything she wanted in a partner. No matter how difficult things had gotten, he hadn't let her down. He'd been there for her, and she wanted the right to do the same for him.

"Harrison?"

"Winter?"

They spoke at the same time and both let out a laugh.

"Ladies first," he said, leaning an arm on the bed, which had him semi-reclining over her legs.

She swallowed hard. "I realize things have changed dramatically from our summer agreement."

He opened his mouth to speak, but she held up her hand.

"Please. I need to do this all at once." Before she lost her nerve.

His gaze narrowed and concern flickered in his eyes. But he nodded. "Go ahead."

"As I said, things have changed since our temporary arrangement, our agreed-upon summer *fling*. And once the shock of me being pregnant wore off, you have stepped up in ways I never expected."

"It was hardly a chore," he said, obviously unable to keep quiet. "I've said it before, but once the notion settled, I knew—"

"No. My turn. You said I could go first," she reminded him. "Anyway. Now that there's no threat, we no longer need to be under one roof. You can go back to your life and I can live mine, and I can fill you in on everything going on with the pregnancy just like I promised I would."

This was hard, and she wasn't making her point well. Her heart was beating so fast that she actually felt the throb in her injured temple. But Harrison had frowned as she started to speak and his expression had morphed into a deeper scowl the longer she went on, which she really hoped was a good omen.

"Is that all?" he asked, a muscle ticking in his jaw.

"No," she whispered. "I *could* do all those things, but I don't want to. I don't want to go home and live separate lives and act like what happened between us these past few weeks has meant nothing to me. Because being with you? It's been *everything*. At least for me."

"Yeah?" he asked, drawing himself upright. "What exactly are you saying?"

Oh, he wasn't going to make this easy, she thought. Because when all was said and done, *she'd* been the one with the walls a mile high. She'd done her best to enjoy him, their intimacy, the sex, their time together while still keeping him at an emotional distance.

"Winter?" he asked, a knowing smile lifting his lips. "Say it," he all but dared her.

Go big or go home, she thought. She could do it, knowing he would catch her. Knowing her heart was safe with him. That *she* was safe with him.

"I'm saying I love you, Harrison Dare."

His eyes somehow lit with happiness and darkened with desire—at the same time. "Well, thank God for that because there was no way I was letting you walk out of this house without telling you the same thing."

"Harrison?" she asked, a certain smile pulling at her lips. "Say it." It was her turn to dare him.

"I love you, Winter Capwell."

The words caused her heart to swell with pleasure.

He clasped her face with his palms and stared into her eyes. "Does this mean you're not going home? You're moving in with me?"

Winter thought about Nikki and Asher, and the stories she'd heard about Nick and Aurora when they'd found each other again, and now she and Harrison. "You Dare men don't waste any time, do you?"

"When we find *the one*, why in the world should we?" His thumb brushed back and forth over her cheek, the feather-light touch arousing her despite the fact that she couldn't do anything about it now. "You still didn't answer me, beautiful. You're not going home, right?"

She smiled wide despite the pain the pulling caused. "Why would I when I'm already there?"

Epilogue

One Year Later

WINTER STOOD WITH Nikki in the back room of Zach and Remy's new establishment in East Hampton, ready to become Mrs. Harrison Dare. And Nikki was ready to become Mrs. Asher Dare. After all they'd been through, they decided a double wedding was exactly what the family needed. And the beachfront restaurant and bar was the perfect place for an intimate family affair. Or as intimate as it could be with all the Dares and Kingstons in attendance.

Although Winter had no desire to look back at the past, she couldn't help but think about the highlights… and lowlights of the last year. Collette pled guilty by reason of insanity and landed herself in a cushy mental institution until the court decided she was competent to stand trial. Because heaven forbid her highness find herself in a state-run hospital like common people who'd committed a crime. The only consolation Winter had was that research, and Zach had assured her that most people who opted for Collette's solution, ended up spending more time incarcerated than those who actually served judge or jury-imposed jail time.

So there was that.

On the happy side, Aurora and Jade had their babies one week apart. Jade and Knox named their little girl Sage. Aurora and Nick also had a daughter. Ellie had been named after Melissa Kingston, who'd taken Aurora into her home after her son, Linc, had found her pregnant at eighteen years old in Florida. Not many women would take in their deceased husband's illegitimate child and Aurora considered Melly the only mother she had. Aside from Serenity, who'd brought her into the Dare fold, of course. Ellie was a mini replica of a now seven-year-old Leah who adored her baby sister.

Winter had her baby five months later. Also a girl, they'd named her Juliana, after Winter's mom. Harrison immediately called her Jules, and it had stuck. His parents couldn't wait to see their sons deal with teenage daughters when the time came and they, along with a still single Zach, were taking bets on the sex of future children that weren't even in existence yet. Girls were the odds-on favorite for all the Dare sons.

"What are you smiling about?" Nikki asked.

Winter turned to her sister, who looked stunning in a beaded sheath dress with a halter neckline, an open back and sparkling tulle liner. Her olive skin was still tan from the summer sun and her long, raven-colored hair hung straight down her back. She was gorgeous and glowed with happiness.

"I was thinking about all the baby girls in the family and their overly protective dads." She lifted her shoulder. "It's just funny."

"It is," Nikki said but she didn't sound like she'd paid attention to the answer and her eyes had taken on a faraway look.

Winter narrowed her gaze. "I was also saying that I'd announce my next pregnancy right before the first dance." She studied her sister who barely registered she'd spoken.

Nikki hadn't replied.

"Aha! I knew you weren't listening." Winter had gone for shock value to see if Nikki was paying attention. She was *not* pregnant again. In fact, she was still waking up at all hours of the night to care for the infant she did have. If her sister *had* heard and believed her, she would be freaking out and jumping up and down with excitement.

"I'm sorry. What did you say?" Nikki asked.

Careful not to touch her face and ruin her meticulously applied makeup, Winter pursed her lips and studied her sister. "You're hiding something."

A little smile lifted Nikki's lips. "Did I tell you how gorgeous you look? I love your hair a little longer and the way it just grazes your shoulders now?" She chef-kissed with her fingers. "Perfecto!"

Winter had searched everywhere for a forgiving style that would hide the post-partum body that still hadn't gone back to normal. And she found the perfect dress. An A-line gown with a v-neckline, patterned leaf appliqués over the sheer lace, a nude liner, and illusion long sleeves.

"Thank you and I love it, but you're deflecting."

A beaming smile lifted Nikki's lips. "Fine. How about I announce *my* pregnancy before the first dance? Since you're not really pregnant anyway."

Winter screamed and danced around, beyond thrilled for her sister and Asher.

Thirty minutes later, the bridal procession began. The triplets played the role of ushers, escorting single women of all ages, and couples to their seats. At nineteen, they were extremely mature in appearance, looking more like well-built men than teenagers and girls swarmed all over them. They were definitely a handful for their parents to handle.

The first person to walk down the aisle was Winter's matron of honor, her mentor, Erin Sawyer. Harrison had opted not to have a best man, so as not to piss off any of his brothers, who were his closest friends.

The bridesmaids came next in deep plum dresses in individual styles that suited their body shapes.

Winter's soon-to-be sisters-in-law and friends were stunning beside their men.

Jade walked with Knox, Aurora held on to Nick's arm, Jessica accompanied her now husband, Derek, and Zach picked up the rear with Raven, who had become Winter's good friend. They were followed by Leah, the most adorable flower girl on the planet.

Finally, the screen that had been set up at the top of the aisle closed so the brides could move closer without being seen by the guests. Canon D by Johann Pachelbel sounded around them, the cue that it was time.

Winter met her sister's gaze and smiled. "Ready?" she asked.

"I can't wait," Nikki murmured.

"Me too." Winter had moved in with Harrison, or rather, she'd never left.

Harrison had her things packed and brought to his apartment. Still, Winter couldn't wait to become Mrs. Harrison Dare because she adored that man and wanted to be his in every way. And she wanted to know he equally belonged to her in the eyes of the law.

"Let's do this," Nikki said as her father, the former senator, hooked one arm in hers to walk her down the aisle.

He kissed her cheek and turned to Winter, slid his other arm into hers and lightly brushed her cheek with his lips.

Then Nikki, the woman who'd been estranged from her father for most of her life, and Winter, who hadn't had a father until last year, waited for the screen to part.

And they walked down the aisle toward the men they loved.

★ ★ ★

Zach

THE WEDDING CELEBRATION continued late into the night. Zach took pleasure in the fact that his siblings had chosen his new bar as their venue. It made him feel a part of things and he liked how his family was always there for each other in varied ways.

"Hey." Remy strode up beside him with two glasses of Dirty Dare Bourbon, handing him one.

"Thanks." Zach took a sip of the sweet, smooth liquor and nodded his approval. Dirty Dare Spirits made a quality drink. "So, are you satisfied with your life change?" he asked his friend and new partner.

Remy inclined his head. "Couldn't be happier." He'd liked working with Zach to find Collette Bettencourt without the rules and restrictions of the NYPD.

So he'd quit the force and joined Zach both in his restaurant business and his PI firm. The one no one in his family knew about until Winter decided if anyone was going to tell the story about Senator Corbin Bettencourt's illegitimate daughter and how his wife had tried to kill her, it should be Winter herself. Because no one else could write the truth with a spin that wouldn't hurt her family. And she'd been correct.

The problem was her story was fascinating and the ultimate clickbait. Was it any wonder the article been picked up by all news outlets?

Winter interviewed everyone involved, and for reasons Zach would never understand, instead of taking credit for Collette's arrest, the police had lauded Zach and Remy for finding her. Once Winter's article had been printed, Zach's past clients had contacted her to sing his praises, precipitating a follow-up piece that also went viral. As a result, Zach's PI business became public and suddenly he had a waiting list of potential clients and fame he didn't want.

Yes, his family liked to think he was a man of mystery with many talents, and sure, he was some of that. But he was also a guy who specialized in finding missing people. Collette had been a pleasure to hunt down because Winter was family, and nobody messed with Zach's family and got away with it. He didn't advertise and only took on people who found him by word of mouth.

His motivation was personal. The week before

prom, Zach's high school girlfriend vanished without a trace. She and her entire family had packed up, leaving an empty house and no note or forwarding address. Zach never heard from her again. Her disappearance had driven him to hone the computer skills that now, years later, he used to help others. Helping people find missing loved ones was emotionally satisfying while the bars fulfilled his entrepreneurial spirit.

Unlike Harrison, or Harrison when he'd been a young actor, Zach preferred to live under the radar. But thanks to the article, women lined up at the bar to meet the wealthy bar owner and famous PI. It was ridiculous. Zach hated the notoriety, so he'd promoted Raven and left the Manhattan bar mostly in her hands. He and Remy had moved to the Hamptons to make the second location a reality.

"Do you ever want what they have?" Remy tipped his head, gesturing to where his siblings and parents slow-danced the night away.

His brothers and sister were coupled off, all with kids, now that Nikki had announced she and Asher had a baby on the way. Zach was equally thrilled for them and just as happy to be fun Uncle Zach.

He shook his head. "Nah." He might have been young, but he'd had his dream girl and she'd left him in the dust.

He was the last man standing. And he liked it that way.

Thanks for reading! What's next?

Check out Zach, the last Dirty Dare brother standing!
Read JUST ONE TEASE!

Want even more Carly books?

CARLY'S BOOKLIST by Series – visit:
https://www.carlyphillips.com/CPBooklist

Sign up for Carly's Newsletter:
https://www.carlyphillips.com/CPNewsletter

Join Carly's Corner on Facebook:
https://www.carlyphillips.com/CarlysCorner

Carly on Facebook:
https://www.carlyphillips.com/CPFanpage

Carly on Instagram:
https://www.carlyphillips.com/CPInstagram

Carly's Booklist

The Dare Series

Dare to Love Series
Book 1: Dare to Love (Ian & Riley)
Book 2: Dare to Desire (Alex & Madison)
Book 3: Dare to Touch (Dylan & Olivia)
Book 4: Dare to Hold (Scott & Meg)
Book 5: Dare to Rock (Avery & Grey)
Book 6: Dare to Take (Tyler & Ella)
A Very Dare Christmas – Short Story (Ian & Riley)

** Sienna Dare gets together with Ethan Knight in **The Knight Brothers** (Dare Me Tonight).*

** Jason Dare gets together with Faith in the **Sexy Series** (More Than Sexy).*

Dare NY Series (NY Dare Cousins)
Book 1: Dare to Surrender (Gabe & Isabelle)
Book 2: Dare to Submit (Decklan & Amanda)
Book 3: Dare to Seduce (Max & Lucy)

The Knight Brothers
Book 1: Take Me Again (Sebastian & Ashley)
Book 2: Take Me Down (Parker & Emily)
Book 3: Dare Me Tonight (Ethan Knight & Sienna Dare)
Novella: Take The Bride (Sierra & Ryder)
Take Me Now – Short Story (Harper & Matt)

The Sexy Series

Book 1: More Than Sexy (Jason Dare & Faith)

Book 2: Twice As Sexy (Tanner & Scarlett)

Book 3: Better Than Sexy (Landon & Vivienne)

Novella: Sexy Love (Shane & Amber)

Dare Nation

Book 1: Dare to Resist (Austin & Quinn)

Book 2: Dare to Tempt (Damon & Evie)

Book 3: Dare to Play (Jaxon & Macy)

Book 4: Dare to Stay (Brandon & Willow)

Novella: Dare to Tease (Hudson & Brianne)

* Paul Dare's sperm donor kids

Kingston Family

Book 1: Just One Night (Linc Kingston & Jordan Greene)

Book 2: Just One Scandal (Chloe Kingston & Beck Daniels)

Book 3: Just One Chance (Xander Kingston & Sasha Keaton)

Book 4: Just One Spark (Dash Kingston & Cassidy Forrester)

Just One Wish (Axel Forrester)

Book 5: Just One Dare (Aurora Kingston & Nick Dare)

Book 6: Just One Kiss

Book 7: Just One Taste

Book 8: Just Another Spark

Book 9: Just One Fling

Book 10: Just One Tease

For the most recent Carly books, visit CARLY'S BOOKLIST page

www.carlyphillips.com/CPBooklist

Other Indie Series

Billionaire Bad Boys

Book 1: Going Down Easy

Book 2: Going Down Hard

Book 3: Going Down Fast

Book 4: Going In Deep

Going Down Again – Short Story

Hot Heroes Series

Book 1: Touch You Now

Book 2: Hold You Now

Book 3: Need You Now

Book 4: Want You Now

Bodyguard Bad Boys

Book 1: Rock Me

Book 2: Tempt Me

Novella: His To Protect

For the most recent Carly books, visit CARLY'S
BOOKLIST page
www.carlyphillips.com/CPBooklist

Carly's Originally Traditionally Published Books

Serendipity Series
Book 1: Serendipity
Book 2: Kismet
Book 3: Destiny
Book 4: Fated
Book 5: Karma

Serendipity's Finest Series
Book 1: Perfect Fit
Book 2: Perfect Fling
Book 3: Perfect Together
Book 4: Perfect Stranger

The Chandler Brothers
Book 1: The Bachelor
Book 2: The Playboy
Book 3: The Heartbreaker

Hot Zone
Book 1: Hot Stuff
Book 2: Hot Number
Book 3: Hot Item
Book 4: Hot Property

Costas Sisters

Book 1: Under the Boardwalk

Book 2: Summer of Love

Lucky Series

Book 1: Lucky Charm

Book 2: Lucky Break

Book 3: Lucky Streak

Bachelor Blogs

Book 1: Kiss Me if You Can

Book 2: Love Me If You Dare

Ty and Hunter

Book 1: Cross My Heart

Book 2: Sealed with a Kiss

Carly Classics (Unexpected Love)

Book 1: The Right Choice

Book 2: Perfect Partners

Book 3: Unexpected Chances

Book 4: Worthy of Love

Carly Classics (The Simply Series)

Book 1: Simply Sinful

Book 2: Simply Scandalous

Book 3: Simply Sensual

Book 4: Body Heat

Book 5: Simply Sexy

For the most recent Carly books, visit CARLY'S
BOOKLIST page
www.carlyphillips.com/CPBooklist

Carly's Still Traditionally Published Books

Stand-Alone Books
Brazen
Secret Fantasy
Seduce Me
The Seduction
More Than Words Volume 7 – Compassion Can't
Wait
Naughty Under the Mistletoe
Grey's Anatomy 101 Essay

For the most recent Carly books, visit CARLY'S
BOOKLIST page
www.carlyphillips.com/CPBooklist

About the Author

NY Times, Wall Street Journal, and USA Today Bestseller, Carly Phillips is the queen of Alpha Heroes, at least according to The Harlequin Junkie Reviewer. Carly married her college sweetheart and lives in Purchase, NY along with her crazy dogs who are featured on her Facebook and Instagram pages. The author of over 75 romance novels, she has raised two incredible daughters and is now an empty nester. Carly's book, The Bachelor, was chosen by Kelly Ripa as her first romance club pick. Carly loves social media and interacting with her readers. Want to keep up with Carly? Sign up for her newsletter and receive TWO FREE books at www.carlyphillips.com.